To all who ride the routes and those w

Our Furzedown, who art in Herne Hill,
New Malden be thy name.
Thy Kingston come; thy Wimbledon,
In Earlsfield as it is in Balham.
Give us this day our Deptford,
And lead us not into Penge station.
But deliver us from Esher.
For thine is the Kennington, the Wandsworth and the
Bromley.
For Erith and Erith,
South Croydon South End.

London folk rhyme (modified).

Hail to the bus drivers, bus drivers, bus drivers,
Hail to the bus drivers, bus driver fam.

American children's rhyme (adapted).

Published by F&M Publications September 2019

www.thecityoverthewater.com
F&M Publications
176C Camberwell New Road
London SE5 0RR

Cover design by Tim Bird
https://www.timothybird.co.uk/

A CIP catalogue record for this book is available from the British Library.

ISBN-13: 978-0-9572134-6-3

Bus Travel in South London

Stories from the city over the water

F&M Publications

Contents

Introduction

In the novel *Wise Children*, Angela Carter wrote of London as two cities divided by a river much in the way there is a Buda and a Pest. I once saw London as a patchwork of off-kilter mirrors; for every Hampstead there is a Dulwich, for every Wapping a Rotherhithe and for every Hammersmith a Putney. However, in my model, where might Brixton – the setting for Carter's novel – reflect? Are there really Middlesex or Essex equivalents for Greenwich, Bermondsey, Tooting or Walworth? In the interests of balance, there are no Kent or Surrey Camden Towns, Clerkenwells or Notting Hills. However earnestly some people in East Dulwich might wish it so.

An alternative view is that, over millennia, settlements including those at the South Work, the Lamb's Harbour and the Deep Ford merged to become Britain's second largest city. A city of millions with a diverse population linked by geography and bus routes around which this collection of stories is set. Few of the stories take place on the bus itself but in each the bus route touches on people's lives or links together locations. The tales are divided between those that might be considered realist and those that could be called magically real. This is a less than perfect dichotomy in South London, which contains a HellRaiser bus stop near the Bricklayers' Arms roundabout, dozens of roving bus preachers and the Peckham Terminator at the Nigel Road bus stop. If these are real – and they are real – how does one designate the uncanny?

Think of what follows as an exploration of a wondrous place full of little known locations with peculiar stories. Nigel, the narrator of Sound of the Suburbs, says:

The number 50 passes through some of South London's lesser known suburbs; once, sitting on the top deck, I had the realisation that very few Londoners live in the city's famous neighbourhoods, whether Chelsea or Knightsbridge, Whitechapel or Peckham. The majority reside in obscure places that most people don't even know exist, never mind have visited. Even fellow south Londoners struggle to recognise Shirley, Furzedown, my own Lark Hall or nearby Springfield, never mind Beulah, Addiscombe or Angell Town. A song from the eighteenth century tried to make sense of all of this:

Sutton for good mutton
Cheam for juicy beef
Croydon for a pretty girl
And Mitcham for a thief.

Consider this collection something of an update from the city over the water for the twenty-first century.

Chris Roberts September 2019

Apologies and thanks

If I've misrepresented any location or, worse, misjudged a bus route, I apologise. Any mistakes in what follows are mine and mine alone. Likewise, any similarities between my fictional characters and people living or dead are coincidental. Both the slang and the bus routes were correct at the time of writing though I'd be the first to acknowledge that few things remain static in the fast paced, ever changing world of Transport for London bus timetabling. The RV1, for example ceased to operate in the summer of 2019 and the 436 stopped crossing the Thames to the north the year before.

Thanks to Grace Fairley of the Big Wide Word for staying patient through the, sometimes painful, editing process and to Julie and Kay for reading some of the early drafts.

A number of asides and footnotes relating to the stories are included at the end of the book and some of these could come under the category of "spoilers" so be careful not to look at them until you've read the tales.

Buses featured

The P13, The 178, The 155, The 185, The 21, The P5, The 47, The 50, The C10, The 356, The 133, The 468, The 196, The 35. The P4, The RV1, The 63, The 315, The 22, The 109, The 159.

The Last of the Gang to Die

I paused to admire the fruit trees in full blossom that lined the path to Eric's place. When he planted them we'd been given less than five years to live, longer than some of them took to fruit. As the prediction of our demise had proved false, Eric must have enjoyed two decade's worth of desserts, spreads, gins and pies.

A soft fruit leaving fruit behind.

I knocked on what was once Eric's door and a man I did not recognise – relative, friend or neighbour, I couldn't say – opened it. In the reception room small groups clustered around tastefully arrayed food and drink.

It was all too much, all too sudden, and I fled for the door with no sense of dignity or decorum through a misty haze of tears and memory. It wouldn't have killed me to visit once in the last twelve years.

I'd barely got halfway back down the path when a lively girl with her hair in plaits took my arm. It was astonishing how much she looked like her mother and I stammered out her name:

"Charlotte?"

"Char Lottay!" She pronounced it with a flourish. "And you are wicked Philip who makes cocktails for impressionable teenage girls!"

She laughed.

"It's one of mummy's favourite stories. How she and a friend bunked off school to visit uncle Eric. He was out but you took them in and, she said, she'd never seen anything so beautiful as the bar you had at number forty-three. All gleaming with different glasses and how you offered them tea then stopped to look to the west and said..."

I picked up the story: "I think I said... 'Well we can legitimately have something stronger don't you agree? The sun's over the yardarm'."

"Mummy tells it that you said the boson is down on the ship's mate."

"Does she? Well, it's possible."

As we passed number forty-three, Charlotte asked whether I'd been back in since I left the estate.

"No. It looks like they've made a nice job of it though. I think the bar was taken by Jamie at thirty-nine." After a while I said, "You know I was angry with your uncle for buying his place with the compensation money he got. I always thought it all should have stayed council but I'm guessing none of these are council anymore, and I'm not sure any council would do what they did for us again."

"Uncle used to call it an estate of the damned. A short-term housing solution for the soon-to-be-departed. I think he wanted to make a permanent statement."

"Yes. He planted the trees as a sort of declaration of war against time and disease."

We turned back to Eric's house, the blossom-laden cherry trees and mature plum trees almost obscuring the entrance where the driveway would be on other houses.

"You do realise I'll probably have to commit murder if anyone bought it and cut them down," I said.

"You do realise that mummy and I have already made that same vow, don't you?"

I looked back at the houses and could almost see things as they'd been when I left twelve years before. Martin hanging out of the window of the house he shared with James. "Admiral" Duncan lounging in a deckchair at forty-nine, the fourth George and third William opposite trying to drag furniture into their upper window and Tony "Lily" Langtry strolling back with shopping and someone he'd clearly recently made the acquaintance of. "Shouting" Joey yelling from behind his permanently open front door.

All gone now. Many went while I was still there. What a variety of ailments there were in the end and, while death was usually a combination of agues, some illnesses stood out for certain people. Martin and the Admiral ultimately succumbed to tuberculosis but Martin also spent some happy time with his eyes, digestive tract and lungs tormented by cytomegalovirus. We all, pretty much, had candidiasis but we lost James to cryptococcal meningitis in 2001. George followed the same year from toxoplasmosis picked up from the aptly named Death Star, his catty companion. William from cryptosporidiosis, Tony from the classic Kaposi's sarcoma. It was hard to tell what finally did for Joey but a pick and mix of passing viruses and opportunistic bacteria could all claim some responsibility.

For me, the 'nineties, which in many ways were the herald of great things, felt like a sneak preview of old age. At the time I was going to more funerals than my parents did. Now I am the age my parents were in the 'nineties I'm a bit less worked up about funerals and considerably more relaxed about saying things out loud that perhaps would be better kept as internal monologues.

Charlotte noticed my change in demeanour and, after a respectful pause, said,

"There's something for you from the estate. Mummy has it."

A woman who could easily have been Charlotte's older sister emerged through the trees and smiled. The smile drew attention both to how wide her mouth was and to the scar down her left cheekbone, the result of a childhood toy-throwing incident involving Eric. Eric had confided that he used to feel really guilty about it, like he'd wrecked a potential modelling career, but later said that it conferred a kind of pirate dignity on his sister.

"I do hope Charlotte's not being a nuisance. She's been dying to meet you."

Charlotte blushed then laughed as I replied. "No more than you!"

The hug was warm and long, and I was shocked at how emotional it made me. Young Dawn, now with her own child who was the same age as when I'd first met her.

"Stand!" Dawn yelled suddenly.

"And deliver!" I rejoined.

Charlotte applauded as between us we executed a passible impersonation of Adam Ant.

"I think that was my favourite ever party. The Shooters' Hill Dandy Highwaymen!"

"Oh Mummy, you always change your mind. You said it was the Horn Fair re-enactment ones the other day!"

"Oh," I said, "did you go to those?"

"Yes I did, but brother Eric was very clear that certain houses were off limits. Including yours! What debauchery took place there, I wonder?"

"Mummy. Show him what you have!"

Dawn reached into her bag and pulled out something

carefully wrapped in a plastic cover.

"I think you might recognise this."

Inside the bag was a white vest.

"Behold!" said Dawn. "The white vest of Bronski Beat!"

"It's said to contain magic powers," laughed Charlotte.

"That's just an old queen's tale!" her mother said, then added, "There are some records too, we found in the attic."

I had no interest in the discs, but the vest had been a source of disagreement. Both Eric and I had laid claim to it and we'd even had a rolling argument about it, which lasted weeks. Though as that was the same time Eric announced he was buying the house it could have been that the two issues got mixed up.

At this point Dawn's husband joined us and, glancing at the vest, said, "Giving away the estate already? I assume it's not worth anything."

Charlotte pulled a face. I recognised the attempt at humour but couldn't respond. He added that he thought it would be nice if, as Eric's oldest friend, I could say a few words to the party.

"Say a few words" is one of those great English euphemisms. Heavy words lightly thrown. What are words worth? How does one encapsulate a life, its impact on yours and others?

Inside, I looked around the group, which was, by turns, sympathetic and expectant. I fought down the urge to be gauche, then relented.

"I understand that in his final years Eric became quite mild and even stopped swearing, that he wished for a curse-free send off." I paused, noting some relief from the vicar and several others.

"Well he can fuck right off on that score."

Tension broke across the room and I told the tale of how twenty or so homosexualists and a few drug addicts found ourselves living in this cul-de-sac near the old Fever Hospital. By the time we all washed up here in Charlton at the end of the 'eighties, some of us had danced our way through disco, punk, new romantic and rave, and a few of us looked surprisingly well on it. The rest looked more like how you might expect. The estate had been planned for pensioners but, instead, in a collaboration between Greenwich and Lewisham Councils, we were moved in.

I told stories of the Horn Fair Parties on St Luke's day, celebrating the anniversary of the Fever Hospital in July and the Highwaymen of Shooters Hill whenever we felt like it. I mean. What else were we supposed to do? We'd been sent there to die!

By the time I stopped the audience was evenly split between the weepers, the laughers and the stunned. Charlotte applauded wildly.

I declined several offers of a lift home. I wasn't keen to stay for the night-time scattering of ashes on the Horn Fair either, though I was amused by the conceit of Eric blowing over the Thames Valley. A part of me wondered what eternity in Lewisham would be like if all the ashes wound up there.

With that thought in mind I got back on the 178 to Woolwich, which had definitely scrubbed itself up in the last decade and some. The military structures still stood out and, as with so much of London, there were clues in the names. Woolwich Arsenal, Gunner Lane, and Ha Ha Road. Of course, there was a store of weapons here, a lane where gunners lived and a folly there. There is no mystique to London. Urban planning is a language, can't you read?

These thoughts didn't help as a distraction. By the time I reached the station I was weeping openly.

A Cyborg's Dream of the P13

When people ask me what I do for a living, I say that I work in anger management and if they press for details, I reply that I help manage it all the way up to rage. Sometimes I think of my job as a sort of dating agency for the furious. The app would be called Tinderbox, putting the concerned and the cross in contact with each other.

I do not offer an opinion; rather, I encourage people to indulge in responses that chime with their prejudices. The goal is to make them feel comfortable in their outrage. From that point others may join the conversation, allowing me to withdraw.

Think of it like dropping a stone into a still pond. I let other people fill in the blanks. Sometimes posting, "I saw a Muslim lady with a full face veil and four kids on the bus" is sufficient to produce a lively response from the trigger-happy, who may reply with:

"More soldiers for Allah."

"I wouldn't recognise Peckham now."

"Watch out mate. Could be anything behind that veil."

"Bet they're on all the benefits while our pensioners freeze."

"That mayor's one of them as well. Just look how the crime rate is going up. London's not safe anymore."

Please allow me to introduce myself. I am Martin Currie or, as I am known to my 65,000 followers, Martincurrie25111415. I travel to work on the 904 bus in Moscow but at work, I ride the P13 bus in South London. In the early days, around 2012, those of us given the London beat referred to ourselves as Boris Bots in a nod to our country of origin and the then mayor's bike hire scheme.

We are linguists, but algorithms and numbers drive our life. We work to a pattern: one personal observation per twenty retweets of mostly unverified political news sources and bloggers, though we acknowledge anyone who engages with us about a story. Our nine-hour days at the office include thirty minutes of research alongside ninety of comfort and meal breaks. I sometimes cut into my lunch to do more exploration and frequently take my work home with me. I have no desire to sound like a poorly schooled call centre operator trained to say, "What about those Emmerdale Enders then? What will they be doing next?"

On one occasion, when we feared exposure, our English teacher remembered the phrase "the man on the Clapham omnibus". The notion that this fictional entity was the barometer of English opinion led him to suggest that we make ourselves appear local by each adopting a different transport route. I chose the P13 (New Cross to Streatham) and have become fascinated with it. Being "on the bus" allows me to freshen up my messages with local observations such as "I see the menu at Popinjay on Bellenden Road has changed".

I would love to visit the Popinjay one day to enjoy a portion of their celebrated Madras crab and I yearn to feel the excitement of the Tulse Hill Tavern on a weekend night. I'm interested to experience the grim allure of the Lordship Lane Estate and the faux rustic charms of Goose Green, to stop off at the exotic sounding Melbourne Grove. My fiancé and I have entered into a fantasy life of shopping at the big supermarket at Dog Kennel Hill or taking in a Dulwich Hamlet football match under the floodlights. We share a dream of a slow holiday travelling across bits of south London that most British people have never heard of.

The work is interesting, steady and offers good prospects, though I barely ever read the trash we retweet. That's all propaganda but – and here is the joy – we do not have to produce any of it ourselves. My grandfather told me how in the old days, his days, at the People's Commissariat for Internal Affairs (NKVD), whole teams might work on a single konspiratsiya. Nowadays the English and Americans produce the goods for us and all we do is direct it to the right audience.

We must be swift and discriminating to pick out different bits of a story that best suits our followers. For left-wingers (never liberals as that's a dead giveaway if you are working the UK threads), it might be a racist attack on a local carnival. For nationalists, a scare story about bushmeat in Peckham might play better.

Research once consisted of looking through the TV guide or football fixtures to make sure we knew what was on and who was playing whom. In this way we might drop in a casual reference without ever expressing an opinion about a match or a character in a show. We honed our skills on Google Maps and – my idea – local restaurant menus and forums. No need to intervene on the latter; just take notes and move on.

My job allows me to indulge my talents for investigation, pleasure in language and acting. Not to mention the technical skills needed to guide one's own bot-crop of non-carbon accounts to a perfect pitch. Like a DJ or a concert pianist, we call up waves of tweets, retweets and comments, endlessly blending and reblending accounts to hit a crescendo. Our goal – aside from linking people together and advancing whatever political line suits us – is to reach the point where the local or even national media picks up on our memes. Though not, obviously, on us.

We are rewarded if we introduce a new word into the discourse and even more if that word enters the Oxford English Dictionary. Punning is difficult in a foreign language, and better people than I are equipped with the skills to do that. One of our better efforts was "remoanstream media" which has seeped out of social media and into people's real-life conversations.

Another goal is to become what we call a franchise. This is where a persona reaches so many followers that it takes more than one person to operate. In that scenario I would train others to be Martin Currie. My fiancé sometimes says that my focus on Martin's realness means she is living with two people. For that reason, it would be nice to retire from Martin and have my apprentices take over.

I do have other talents I wish to explore. Music has always been important in my family. My mother was a fan of American pop music and I grew up to the sounds of Bob Dylan and Johnny Cash, the Beach Boys and the Eagles. It is not what I listen to now but it did inspire me to write a song celebrating my favourite bus route. It is called I met my dream on the P13. When it is finished, I might record it and upload it, quietly and under another assumed name to one of the Transpontine blogs.

If you're planning a leisurely journey west
Get the bus that's the most fuss, that's the best
Go to Mount Ephraim on the P13

It winds from New Cross to Streatham Hill
Takes hours to get there all the way
Go through Goose Green on the P13

From my father, who used to watch the Dynamos play in Europe, I learned a different song, one that English teams sang. The words are: "We are here and we are there, we are bloody everywhere."

I take this as my mantra and, while we may not be on your route just yet, you can be assured that we are definitely on the buses.

Liebe Astrid

The first time Lena and I visited Anna's flat we took the bus. The wrong bus, as it turned out, even if it was the only one that stopped directly outside her block.

"You got the P5? Elephant and Castle to Wandsworth Road in under two hours. I won't put the kettle on just yet," said Alfred, Anna's partner, when we called him to say we'd be late.

After the P5 finally dropped us off and rolled away aggressively on its low centre of gravity to Coldharbour Lane, Alfred ushered us in and listed in a deadpan voice the other buses we could have taken from Elephant that, as he put it, "aren't proper round the houses". He smiled and added, "or the train is only five minutes from the Elephant and it doesn't take much longer to walk from Loughborough Junction Station to here. Still, you're here now. Tea?"

Alfred busied himself in the kitchen and Lena and I gazed out of the tenth floor living room windows. The Loughborough Park Estate was tall, skinny and brutal, like a piece of Minsk or East Berlin had been deposited in London. This felt apt, as we were there to film part of a documentary about Anna, who had been a notorious left-wing agitator and had lived on the estate incognito since the 1970s, in exile from Germany.

Anna's real identity didn't become apparent to Alfred until after she died, when he had contacted her family including Lena, her niece. It was only then that Lena realised that her aunt, who had been missing and presumed dead, had in fact been in London for four decades. Alfred had been with Anna till the end of the illness that killed her.

He explained to us over tea and biscuits, "She was just Anna. Tall, beautiful and ironically funny, and whatever she'd been before was a bloody long time ago. When I met her, she was another transpontine living life on the sunny side of the Thames."

I had to look up the word transpontine (it meant over the bridge) later. Lena and I just nodded and he continued.

"I know you want to film here but you're going to have to be quick as the council want this flat back. No problem storing

18

things at my place, but I reckon you've two weeks maximum here."

He paused and chuckled.

"And you've only got that because I tore a proper strip off an uppity housing officer. I called her a grave robber with no sense of decency, given how recently Anna had been laid to rest."

He looked at Lena and said, "I'm sorry you never got to meet her or go to the funeral but, I have to admit, getting you over here wasn't my first priority."

Alfred indicated a chest of drawers and said; "There are some papers in there, a few documents, photos and loads of letters, in German so I can't read them. Most of them are addressed to someone called Astrid. I wondered whether Anna ever intended to send the letters, or they were like a diary or," his accent switching from South London cockney to something noticeably more BBC presenter, "the historical record."

After Lena had received the news of her aunt's death, we had gathered together memoirs, academic studies and news clips. Now we had Anna's own writings, kept in a drawer in cardboard folders arranged by date. We planned to use some of these in the film.

I smiled back at Alfred. "Now you know there is a historical record, is this not something you want to be a part of?"

Alfred firmly shook his head. "Be asking me about someone I never knew. No point in that, is there?" Alfred added that Lena was welcome to anything in the wardrobe but there were a couple of knick-knacks he wanted to keep.

I had to look up knick-knacks later as well as, for an awful moment, I thought he meant knickers.

After we'd sorted the papers into piles Lena went into the bedroom to look at her aunt's clothes, occasionally emerging with items to show me. This gave me an idea of how we would film some of the letter extracts, if Lena was agreeable and Alfred come to that.

We selected four letters we could easily link to photographs and that covered, as far as anyone knew, Anna's romantic relationships. The first entry we chose was 9 November 1976 and Lena wore leather trousers and a black tee shirt to read to camera.

Dear Astrid,

After months of no contact I received a note from one of the comrades in Brixton who helped get me this flat. It was signed "Tom", one of the schwulen from a squat in Mayall Road where I stayed for a week. The note was an invitation to a punk (which was not a term I knew) concert at the Mucky Duck pub and suggested, arrogantly I thought, that I wear my leather trousers.

I was glad I wore them because the wind bit at me even on the short walk under the railway bridge and past the drab Victorian townhouses to Coldharbour Lane. Tom was in the back room near to a low stage and stood out in his flared trousers and feather haircut. Next to him was another man who, in drainpipe jeans, a black t-shirt and leather jacket, blended much more easily with the crowd, as did I in my leather trousers.

Tom's friend was called Gerald, or Gerry as he quickly corrected it to, and after ten minutes of small talk between the three of us Gerry muttered "time for action" and strode onto the stage where a band was noisily tuning up. Tom leaned over and said,

"I went to a private school with him in Surrey. Not that he'd ever admit that now!"

The prep school boy from Surrey looked wild as with a crash the performance began. Song thrashed into song, all angry spiky denunciations of unfairness, ironic comments on everyday life, and the poor conditions for the young and dispossessed. Many in the audience flailed around in an aggressive dance and I noticed that Gerry, directed much of his performance at me.

"Er ist total geil," I whispered to Tom, who nodded that he understood the sentiment, if not the words.

Gerry sang at least one song twice but still was offstage in half an hour. His energy excited me and the fact that he had picked up a microphone where I had reached for the Molotov; he the lyric, I the revolver. He looked so innocent and yet so potent, so vulnerable and yet brave, my first English lover, the punk rocker.

I cropped my hair and threw out the floral tops. I bought tight trousers and pointed shoes. No one would recognise me now!

It took Lena several attempts to get into the character of the aunt she'd never known but, as was clear from the photos, closely resembled.

Our second choice was from nearly a decade later, 19 September 1985. Anna (Lena's) look was still rock and roll but with better jewellery and bigger hair, made possible for Lena after we'd taken a trip to one of Brixton's remaining wig bazaars.

Dear Astrid,

Both sides are better equipped than in the last riots. From up here I can spot the shift change as people filter through the estate, some with small prizes and others with injuries.

On the second night the police set up a command post at the junction of Coldharbour Lane and Shakespeare Road. Sometimes the buses are escorted one way, sometimes another. Occasionally they, and cars and people are turned back altogether. Through my open window I hear the disturbances, smell, and sometimes see the fires to the west.

I find the excitement outside oddly relaxing after eight hours on the wards with Claudette and Doreen and the rest of the largely Caribbean, or of Caribbean origin, nurses at Kings Hospital where I worked.

I cannot properly relax though without a smoke and when I reach for a cigarette I find both the packet and my emergency tobacco pouch empty. Shops in London shut early and there are no corner imbiss so I jog down the ten flights and cross the yard to the Hero of Switzerland pub. There I can use their cigarette machine or buy some tobacco under the counter, as the English say. Secretly, my middle-class self prefers the casual illegality of these purchases and much else about pub life, from the meat man who sells "hooky" beef to the "lock-ins". I sometimes think I should write an alternative London travel guide with such useful terms in it.

Outside I am crossing back to the block when I hear a young man call.

"Aunty, aunty! Here!"

I recognise Doreen's nephew Michael, who is a regular

presence at his real aunt's flat on Milkwood Road where he wolfishly downs fritters and anything else Doreen could produce. Michael's mother lives over in Harlesden and, in Doreen's opinion, never feeds the boy properly.

"Aunty... here."

Michael is supporting a man of about my age. Under the streetlight the man look strangely bleached and I can see a dark patch on his white t-shirt under his shoulder.

Michael says, "I was taking him fea aunty Doreen's but Babylon block the Lane."

I look at his friend.

"Bring him up to my place. I can dress the wound."

And so arrives on my doorstep my second English lover, Desmond. Some echt English people might question it, with his dark skin and oriental eyes but he is far more roast beef than rice and beans and, though he might talk patois in public, in private, with me, he talks a genial Liverpudlian.

We tried to contact Desmond's relatives with no success but did receive a very polite response from the Michael Williams, now Doctor of Philosophy. He wished us all the best but revealed the sad news that his aunty Doreen had died a dozen years previously. He said some very kind things about Anna, which made Lena cry and the next piece, from 12 April 1992 was a chance for Lena to move on as much as Anna did.

Dear Astrid,

It is the weekend of my 40th birthday. Alles gute für mich! Some of the "girls" from my work in the college on Barrington Road insisted that we go out to dance last night. I say girls – they are, it is true, mostly younger than I, but none will see thirty again. I think of myself sixteen years earlier at my first punk gig. Lat night I felt like Merton dressed as Lambeth, I felt old. I was a bit wary because they were taking me to a venue that played salsa, mambo, world music. At home as I got ready, I played my "indy", my punk, my reggae and my Bowie.

Instead of leather pants I wore a cool silk trouser suit, hair up and full slap. I love this term. Desmond's relatives, the female ones anyway, used to be appalled at how little make up

I wore. They'd like me more now. We still write and, more rarely, call, and there are cards for my birthday from Liverpool and Jamaica, a reminder of both my loss and theirs. Eighteen months since sickle cell disease did its worst. Had we been married I'd be a widow.

In my widow's weeds I stood up, stretched, lit some charge and inhaled deeply. Then I headed out.

There were two music rooms at the venue. One was cavernous, lively and Latin, whilst the other was smaller, laid back and played African and West Indian tunes. Signs that prohibited the smoking of cannabis were ignored. I relit my joint and looked about. Five years with Desmond had taught me not to be desperate in my movements but rather be gentle and groove to the tune. I took to the floor and stepped softly around it, able to be in control and my coolness acted as a deterrent to, at least, some of the men.

I felt his eyes on me before I heard the voice. A gruff South American inflected English but clearly spoken and, given that I am nearly two metres tall in heels, it came from below.

"You dance very well. Like a Latin. May I join you? My name is Alejandro."

He did not dance particularly "like a Latin" if that was what he meant by sensual and forceful, but he had an easy and unhurried way of moving. He also had, as the English say, a few years on me.

The downside of revealing Anna through her relationships with men was not lost on us but this structure did provide a strong framework, a timescale and shifts of tone in the letters that enabled us to show how Anna's life moved on. Even though the way she looked changed, Anna's character remained the same; clever and kind but always a bit detached.

Astrid aside, there were surprisingly few references to Anna's former comrades in Germany, and neither was there any indication that Anna ever tried to contact them. It was as if Anna had gone native and, like a method actor, taken on her new role so completely that, rather than being an attempt to hide or fit in, it had become her. She just became Anna in London.

The final letter we selected was from 10 October 2012, five years before Anna died. It was triggered by the death of "Astrid". In it,

Anna reflected on her former life but, in doing so, closed the door on it forever. It was a door she never opened to her family at all, which upset Lena, who swore and cursed her aunt, in part for Anna's detachment, in part in anger.

For the older Anna we needed the help of a professional make-up artist as Lena got into the character of Anna one last time.

Dear Astrid,

Your death made the papers here, at least the broadsheets, but you and I are history class, the rich girls who became terrorists. Other women travel to fight today and I'm not expected to understand their struggle, religiously inspired, as ours was political. I wonder if they will live in captivity or liberty, or in a hidden life like the one I have had in a strange land.

I suppose I always knew that you'd never read these words; now I really know you won't it still is a shock. I hoped that if I wrote things down, with you as my confessor, it might help. I think, too, how actions have consequences and, most of all, how young we were. After Die Mauer fell I wanted to reach out to our former comrades in the DDR but Desmond was ill and what possible good would it have done?

I did see one old friend early this year. Tom was in Brixton market outside a Thai restaurant with his partner, husband rather, and they both looked distinguished with their polite beards. Like me he never left the area but there are all kinds of divides and we moved in different orbits around the same Brixton sun. He owns a house at the Herne Hill end of Railton Road. A long way from the Mayall Road squat socially and politically but, I calculate, less than 300 metres geographically.

Tom introduced me to the lido in Brockwell Park, in which I can swim for free now I am 60. This is where I met my latest and I think – I hope – last English lover. He is proper, as they say here. He has "no side". His name is Alfred and he is a carpenter. He is steady and funny and, after Alejandro, tall. I am happy. I am on this journey as you have ended yours and now, looking down at the funny little local bus that takes ages to go nowhere in particular, I feel content that my life has only minor dangers and I move through ordinary places that I can, at last, call home.

Anna's home was returned to the council two days after we finished the recordings. I wondered whether the new occupants would be interested to know that the previous tenant had been a member of one of the most notorious terrorist groups of the twentieth century. I doubted that there would be any sort of plaque to chronicle the fact, however keen local history groups might be of such a "celebrity" endorsement of area.

White Man on the Clapham Omnibus

On the evening of December the third, 1980, Martin "Oswald" Jones stood on the balcony of his flat above Clapham South tube. His (late) father's uniform pinched a bit around the leg and he'd had to leave the top two buttons undone at the neck, but he felt he had to mark his namesake Oswald Mosley's passing somehow. It's what his parents would have wanted.

He recalled his fifteen-year-old self looking down from the same spot and seeing the first West Indians arrive in the shelters on the Common. There had been two hundred of them; now there were two hundred thousand across the city. He looked north towards Brixton whence those first arrivals had left to register at the Labour Exchange on Coldharbour Lane. How different London might be if the Labour Exchange had been in Battersea.

On a professional level Martin didn't dislike black people and, as an employee of London Transport, worked alongside, supervised and even, as a shop steward, represented them. In fact, he preferred interceding for them sometimes over fat idle layabouts of his own pedigree. He knew neither his father nor his mother who had, ironically given her politics, died the day Margaret Thatcher was elected, would understand.

Looking out across the darkness of the park Martin remembered his mum's love of Clapham Common, her eager voice gushing.

"We'd go, as a family, to the ponds to feed the ducks! It was such a treat. I imagine children today would sneer at that. I expect they'd find it fuddy duddy and silly with their transistors and television. Such noise!"

Martin usually smiled non-committedly, which allowed her to catch her breath and continue.

"When I was young before the war, that's the first war, the people were so smart on a Sunday and all the houses through Kennington and the Oval into Stockwell were ever so clean and proper looking. Not like today, I mean, some people never wash their steps."

Warming to her theme, she carried on. "Then it was proper Clapham with all the shops bright and painted but shuttered on Sunday except for the tea rooms near the Common and we could, if your grandfather was feeling extravagant, have an ice cream. Oh I should like an ice now."

In the early 1970s his mother moved into a retirement community in SE17, four streets from the house she had been brought up in, but she missed the Common terribly. In consequence, as she preferred not to use the tube, Martin spent many of his weekends accompanying her on the 155 bus to her old flat, which was now his.

During her final illness, when she was an in-patient at St Georges Tooting, Martin would take the 155 through the "Gateway to the South" that is Balham to visit her. The journey was enlivened for Martin by memories of his mother's enthusiasm for the beautiful Art Deco Du Cane Court on the High Street. Like many others in the area, she thought that Hitler's generals had earmarked the building for their own after the planned invasion of England, which was why it was spared wartime bombing. She was in a minority, however, in her belief that Du Cane Court would be improved by the presence of Nazi officers and swastika flags.

If the trips to and from St Georges' were upsetting for Martin, as he never knew whether each one would be the last, then the earlier ones from the Elephant had been unsettling, if predictable. He and his mum would walk across the Walworth Road – White Walworth, as his mum called it – then turn right at the derelict looking public wash houses and on down Crampton Street on the edge of the Pullens Estate. His mother might stop to chat with an acquaintance or nod with approval at any National Front graffiti or passing skinheads.

"They're such good boys" she'd intone. "Look how smart they are! Mr Mosley would have approved of those shiny big boots."

She'd pause and savour the thought.

"There were lots of comrades on Crampton Street. The reds used to meet at the Giraffe pub but the Queen's Head was ours. We used to chase them off up towards Kennington and give that horrid little Yid who ran the shop on Amelia Street a hard time."

Scowling at passing West Indians, she'd shift back decades to when "the Peelers would come bustling down from Carter Street to prevent the traitors getting a proper kicking. Can't understand why the police protected them as they caused most of the crime."

The journey up from the bus stop opposite the London Park Hotel, especially after the Oval, inevitably followed a pattern. His mother would tut at the state of once prosperous Stockwell and start her "spot the nationalist graffiti" game. Two points for an NF, ten for a National Front, twenty for the rarer 1950s classic KBW (Keep Britain White) and one for the ubiquitous "Wogs Out!"

One day his mother was enjoying a grumbling monologue about morality (decline of), backbone (lack of), immigration (too much of) and standards (removal of) until they got on the bus at Newington Butts and there were no seats on the lower deck. Near the door were three West Indian lads sprawled over six seats, doing no harm, just being a bit loud and self-absorbed. Martin's mother bristled but before anything emerged from her mouth beyond a low hiss, something quite miraculous happened. A vision in a uniform descended from the upper deck. She was short with unruly hair emerging from under her cap but the rest of her outfit was immaculate. She clocked the lads, as well as Martin and his mum, and went into action.

"Delroy Philips, your mother brought you up better than this. Can you not see the nice lady there who needs a seat?"

Delroy looked suitably embarrassed but his friends were about to start an argument when the clippie turned on them and said.

"You have feet on seat? Off now. You. I know your Aunty and she will be hearing of this, show some respect for yourself, others and the London Transport bus." She added more gently. "Plenty seats up top, now off you go."

And they did.

Martin, who had been raised by extremists, was an appeaser at heart and seized his moment to smooth things over.

"Mum, look – there are some seats here now."

His mother's mouth moved but nothing came out as she sat down and stared with as much dignity as she could muster at the West Indian conductress. It was clear to Martin that his mother's confusion was quite profound. Elegance, manners and efficient politeness had undone her and it wasn't until they reached Fentiman Road that his mother, no doubt cheered by spotting an actual Mosley lightning bolt flash (worth 50 points on the fascist I-Spy scorecard), regained the power of speech and, with it, the ability to change the subject.

"I see that provincial grocer's daughter is doing rather well for herself," she said as they passed through the dowdy villas of Stockwell and the new build estates. Margaret Thatcher posed a dilemma for Martin's mum. She was both white and female, not to mention right wing, but she was also about to destroy the best chance the far right in Britain had had in decades by taking their constituency. Mentally his mum totted up another three NFs and one National Front but failed to notice her son's own dilemma as his eyes tracked the clippie's movements and easy manner.

The bus conductress was light skinned and when she smiled, which was often, her teeth were as perfect as the rest of her small featured face. She had two small hooped gold earrings but no gold hoop on her left hand. Her manner was friendly and concerned, more that of a nurse than a bus conductress, as she chatted to her passengers and enquired after their family and health. Martin was wondering how he'd never seen her before when an old gentleman with a white dog said,

"Early for you Rita isn't it? Did they change the shifts?"

She nodded before reaching over to press the stop bell, and Martin caught a scent of jasmine. Suddenly his mother, who had dozed off, woke up and yelled "Britain awake!" to which the conductress leaned over and said.

"Well you are now, dear."

Fortunately, they had reached their stop near the Windmill pub so after a brief exchange of glances with Rita, Martin and his mother got off to walk the length of the Common, past the ponds and bandstand to his flat.

So it went every Sunday, Martin and his mum becoming two of Rita's regulars, Martin gladly, his mum tight-lipped. When his mum was taken into St George's it was just Martin who rode the bus, with Rita his confidant, confessor and later, much later, lover.

From the balcony, Martin heard the phone ring. It was Rita.

"Bit late off the shift. You still want me to come over?" After he'd said yes, she asked, "You wearing your uniform? It's terribly smart on you."

He laughed and said yes before putting the receiver down. Looking out once more over the Common at the shelter, in his guilty mind's eye he could see the old graffiti that read "Perish the Negroes", which his mum had encouraged him to write more than thirty years before.

The Lad Who Walked Alone

The north side of Lower Marsh Street was barely recognisable from only a decade ago, since when it had been glassed and framed and boxed out of all individuality. The entrance to the graffiti pleasure park – ask about our spray and display parties – was arched four floors up with bars, boutiques and flats. Canary Wharf had come to Waterloo. Margaret Thatcher, may she rot in pieces, would have been pleased.

My bus cruised on, through narrower, virtually car-free roads, which it shared with cycles of varying types. Thatcher once said, "When I see a man in his thirties waiting at a bus stop I know that man has failed in life". Yet I was still swanning about my old patch on the 159 in my sixties, en route to St Thomas'. No one drove in this city anymore. Why on earth would you?

The omnibus may have survived but precious few of what one former resident of the Marsh area described as "Dark Satanic Mills" had been left un-loft-converted. Nor had the neat little library or any of the three bookshops, including the one I worked at, survived. They were all part of a perfect little street of shops near the centre, just adjacent to the thunder of commuter trains. I did all my Christmas shopping there, in the bookshops or one of the two quality retro stores, four boutiques, two jewellery shops and transport memorabilia emporium. One December I purchased a selection of Mersey Rail timetables from the 1980s for my Uncle Ray. These proved a mixed success, as my Auntie Joan complained he just used them to reminisce about his hooligan forays and benders on the Wirral.

Alongside the shops, pubs, takeaways, cafes and supermarket stood The Beach. Beachers, or Bum Beach to the rude, was one of London's oldest male saunas, going back to the days when the phrase "gay bachelor" could still be used without everybody smirking. Not that anyone smirked about the boy.

I first heard of the lad in the red Levi Strauss popover through that conduit of London lore, the taxi driver. Like other people, London cabbies made a link between me and "the boy" because he was popularly believed to be a Scouser, though no one, at least no one telling the tale in the early millennium, had heard him speak. Many claimed to have seen him; in fact, I wondered if I hadn't seen him myself once or twice, outside the store or leaning on the railings by the tunnel under the station. Slight frame, Lois jeans, Adidas stitched leather holdall, Puma trambs and a brown Perry Boy flick.

Everyone seems to remember the Levi Strauss hoodie. I may have sketched in the other fashion details from Uncle Ray, as trends for trainers, jeans and jackets changed with bewildering rapidity in the city by the Mersey after football supporters' European "shopping" trips.

One account had the lad marooned at Waterloo on his way back from such a European adventure. An alternative had him not going home after being sickened by the events at Heysel; another that he lost his love at Hillsborough. Whatever the dates, everyone agreed that he had a connection to Liverpool and football. He hung around Waterloo, slept rough near the infamous Bullring and did odd jobs. Nobody ever connected him outright to the South Bank rent scene but he did spend many nights at Beachers, where the owners sometimes permitted him to nod off overnight, at his own risk, in the sauna area.

The three owners initially thought he had overdosed but then it became clear that he had fallen and knocked his head. Too late to take what was obviously now a corpse across to St Thomas' and there were no friends or family to contact. In a bad period to be gay in Britain, they believed headlines like "dead boy found in sex sauna" might deal their business a blow and, while Beachers had a few MPs as regulars, they would not help if the story broke.

One of the owners suggested moving the body elsewhere, using that section of their clientele who had links to London's criminal aristocracy. The other two were scared the villains would forever be able to trade on the favour owed. None of them seriously considered dumping the body themselves, via a trip with spades to Epping Forest. A solution presented itself when they remembered that one of the hot tubs in the complex needed refurbishment, and they buried the lad underneath it.

Witnesses from the night, or more likely early morning, of his death were unlikely to be reliable given the state of some and secretiveness of others. When no questions had been asked after a month the owners calmed down. However it is worth recording that none of them ever used the refurbished hot tub or allowed contractors to conduct its maintenance.

Stories gradually seeped out about a lad who was sometimes seen – barely glimpsed through the steam – in the showers or the sauna, and there were sightings on the Marsh itself. By the 'nineties, when the legend had become established, a local café owner told me about it.

I asked him why no one ever reported anything to the police and he said simply,

"Well no one likes a grass do they? Anyway, it might not be true. The lad might just have gone back home or met his end some other way nearby. There were more dodgy goings on back then and all kinds of crimes went unreported."

I suggested it could have been murder but he just shrugged and said, "Young lad, no money, living rough, Scouser – no disrespect to you mate, but to all intents and purposes a foreigner. He's around for a while then goes. Hardly worth getting steamed up about is it? Poor provincials came to make their fortune here and not all of them were welcome."

London always attracted internal migrants and many, like me, earned our gelt and moved to the roomier suburbs. There were more jobs then than in the 'eighties. Perhaps an equivalent lad today might have found employment at the Graffiti Arch Experience or one of the other attractions that drive the London economy.

When Beachers was finally demolished, I scanned the papers in anticipation of a "mystery body". Nothing emerged apart from some evidence of an old graveyard, possibly Saxon, and some artefacts from the Georgian era. Conceivably the chlorine in the pools made the boy corrode away over the decades. Or maybe he never existed.

Returning from St Thomas', I saw how the new buildings by the South Bank tower over the Marsh and as the bus passed the turning to Hercules Road I thought of William Blake. He watched the area change from semi-rural to industrial, just as I saw it go from ordinary to banal. I've no idea what he'd think of that transformation but he'd some very strong words about the one he witnessed:

Thro' midnight streets I hear
How the youthful Harlot's curse
Blasts the new-born Infant's tear
And blights with plagues the Marriage hearse.

The boutique hotel erected on the site of Beachers provoked a cheerier ditty:

They've shut the sex sauna and made things la di da and things ain't what they used to be.

They most certainly are not – except that possibly out there, when the lights of the office computers dim and the bars close on the old Marsh, a lad still walks. Alone.

New Cross Roads and Friendly Streets

"Off out dancing?"

Denise adjusted her umbrella to see the Plumsteads cheerily waving at her from upstairs. A re-angled drip went down her neck.

"Hardly," she yelled back. "Can't even face cycling in this."

Denise was dressed as for a night out, at least as much of a night out as she had these days, and even if there was no music or lights there would be people and chatting.

The rain lashed against the old Hatcham Liberal Club opposite and the wind shifted at a decent clip off the river from Deptford. The building was now residential but still dominated the street. The Plumsteads had met there, he up from Peckham, she from Deptford, both mods who bonded over the ska sounds of the late 1960s. A decade later they moved in opposite the club and watched as the punks traipsed through its doors. No more dancing on the parqueted floor, thought Denise, and reflected that if it had still been the working men's debating club it had started out as, she'd be spared a trip to Lewisham on the number 21.

Hatcham itself had vanished as neighbouring New Cross usurped its place on the maps but in the Domesday Book it was recorded as Hacheham, meaning "home of a man named Hæcci". Nine villagers lived there and there was sufficient woodland for three pigs. Denise liked the idea of three little piggies, as the wind gusted about and tried its best to take down the houses. Hatcham was in Surrey and Lewisham had once been in Kent but county boundaries meant little today compared to more pressing divisions between manors to do with waiting lists, drugs retailing and cultural identity.

These modern distinctions involved shifting complex fashions, whereas Denise longed for simplicity of cause, action and reaction, a time when left was right and right was wrong. The past represented clarity for her. Denise knew whose side she would have been on in 1865 during the strike against Mr George England's Hatcham Iron Works where the Hong Kong City Chinese restaurant now stood. Likewise in 1926, in what the Kentish Mercury described as "Rowdyism in New Cross", she would have been with the two thousand pickets blockading the entrance to London's largest tram depot.

Denise sighed as she reached Ilderton Road and climbed to the top deck of the 21. She'd never been a fan of the bendy buses but these replacements were a terrible waste of money. Water streamed down the windows and she had to rub them to see out to the supermarkets, station and shops on the run up to New Cross. Not far behind the buildings was Clifton Rise where in 1977 the National Front rallied. The planned march by the 500 extreme right wingers through Lewisham was prevented by thousands of left wingers and local people. This had been Cable Street for the double-denim age, a stand against evil and a point in time when wickedness was halted.

Lewisham '77 exercised a kind of juju on Denise and was one of the things that had attracted her to the area. She'd arrived in the 1990s in time for the golden age of the Venue club with its Brit Pop edge but, by the time New Rave – New Cross's other claim to musical fame – emerged, she had developed a fondness for bluegrass and divided her spare time between playing that and politics.

Denise had worked for the great leaps forward of 1997 and 2000 with the elections of Tony Blair and Ken Livingstone, and had been one of the thousands thronging the South Bank in the dawn hours in '97, singing "things can only get better". Bright eyed, full of joy, holding hands for the first, and as it turned out, last time with Clarissa. They'd swayed along the Thames, kissed and, briefly under the leafy protection of some bushes in Bernie Spain Gardens, gone rather further. It had felt liberating, like anything was possible.

She wasn't alone then. She was part of something bigger. In an act of remembrance, she wrote "Portillo" on the bus window after the defeated Conservative MP, Michael Portillo. Then, slightly embarrassed, wiped it clear again.

Denise's workplace, Lewisham College, appeared on the right and she recalled her union walking out in support of workers at another college two years previously. The other college had gone on strike for months while she and others tweeted in support, donated money and waved flags. The strike failed but it made Denise realise how unusual it had been to hear the phrase "all-out indefinite strike" in the media. One just didn't any more.

She didn't hear from Clarissa either.

Ghosts! Denise thought as the bus passed the site of the old Elephant House on Lewisham Way, its gothic splendour replaced by a modernist block on the downhill trajectory towards Lewisham. The old house had been built in the mid-nineteenth century, gaining its name from a giant elephant's head sculpture that once hung ominously from the front of it. Denise had been to a squat party there, where she began a brief affair with a mature student. More ghosts!

She banished the past and focused on the present. There had been much excitement at her work about the night's meeting and, though an unreliable guide, the Facebook attendee list was impressive. Denise was thrilled that she'd know people, all there for a common cause, and maybe she would meet new folk or even meet someone. She banished that hope but felt positive as the bus drew up at the bottom of Loampit Hill.

The venue was a former British Home Store secured for the night by hipster supporters of the Movement For Change. The Leader's ability to galvanise the young as well as older lefties like herself impressed Denise. She waved at some colleagues and fell in with them as the crowd thickened and funnelled into the pop-up village hall.

The furnishings were basic but in one corner there was a bar selling soft drinks, warm and cold, and opposite was another taking "donations" for a glass of something stronger. Denise made a contribution for a red wine and took a seat. Elsewhere, groups of students seemed happy to take up positions on the floor around the periphery.

The mood was earnest but upbeat after the warm-up acts of union officials, young party members and one long-term ally of the Leader. Denise relaxed and looked about her. By her estimate and experience of counting assemblies at work, there were more than four hundred people in the room and most communities were represented, even if the majority were white, and it appeared to her that students and public-sector employees made up the majority.

Denise applauded enthusiastically as the Leader stepped up to the microphone and she was impressed at how ordinary he was in the flesh. He was, to Denise, deliciously unflashy and somehow real. The Leader spoke calmly in a low clear voice and built up to elicit a response, using his hands to beat out a strong point.

"We are accused of denying their economic reality; yet all the time they deny our real poverty."

The audience responded wildly and the Leader followed up with more. He focused on those in the hall and instilled in them the belief that they, in the hall, in the movement, were correct.

"There is nothing more powerful than an idea whose time has come and, comrades, we can be that idea!"

Cheers erupted around Denise as about her people were being told what they wanted to hear, and she heard what she needed to. It felt like the certainty she craved, and it wasn't just her. There were shiny eyed career woman, young men flushed with emotion and an elderly chap waving his cap like a football supporter in an old newsreel.

"On the 25th of November, seventy-two years ago today, a shop much like this one in nearby New Cross was hit by a V2 rocket fired by the Nazis. One hundred and sixty-eight people died. Thirteen more people died in a fire started by racists thirty-five years ago; and next year will mark the fortieth anniversary of the heroic uprising that stopped the fascists marching in Lewisham."

The Leader paused.

"We have a proud history of opposition to fascism and people have died here because of it. We must not, with their talk of austerity and globalisation, let the new oppressors or their media allies deceive us. We must not let them mislead us. We must believe in a better country; we must fight for it and we will achieve it!"

People whistled, stamped and cheered as the Chair grabbed the microphone and yelled, "The leader of the largest political party in Europe and with your help the next Prime Minister!"

Her face flushed, Denise felt surrounded by joy and belonging, and she clapped till her hands were sore. The ghosts of 1997 had reappeared, but they seemed friendlier and differently dressed. Behind them she could sense her younger self, an eager teenager voting for the party at her first election. In her mind's eye, past election campaigns and political struggles flashed by, along with haircuts, badges, coats she had loved and places she had been. Then someone touched her arm and broke her reverie. Did she fancy going to the pub?

Denise left with them and outside there were songs, not about things getting better but about righting wrongs; not about governance but vengeance. Where was the love, Denise wondered, as she listened to people sing.

> *"Build a bonfire, build a bonfire.*
> *Put the Tories on the top.*
> *Put the Blairites in the middle*
> *And burn the bloody lot!"*

Someone shouted, "Red Front!" and no one laughed, at least not ironically.

Denise felt the most awful deflation as the mood shifted from the warm optimism of her journey there and in the hall to the ugliness and cold of the street outside. She changed her mind about the pub and got on the bus and pondered why the first half of the sentence about being the largest party was greeted more loudly than the second. As if that was the most important thing.

The rain stopped as she walked up Queens Road and turned into the drive. The Plumsteads were just in front of her with their Scottie dog, Elsa.

As she stepped into the shared hall, Mr Plumstead asked about the dance.

"Well", said Denise, "we certainly took a jump to the left."

To which the Plumsteads chorused in unison.

"That'll mean a step to the right."

"Probably" said Denise, glumly, as she turned the key in the lock.

The Tale of the Raven and of the Kat

Once upon a time, when the lights shone bright at a crossing point of the Ravensbourne river, two girls shared a room above an alley off Catford Broadway. Due to an administrative error on the council's part, the alley was also called Catford Broadway and, if you strained your neck from the top deck of the 47, you could still just catch sight of it.

Like countless others, the pair were lured by the exotic excitements of Catford's cinemas, theatres and film studios. One of the girls, it was said, had fled a life of destitution, prostitution and an institution. The other, it was claimed, was a foreign princess whose whole family was murdered by revolutionaries. One of them was called Katherine Ford and the other Raven Bjorn. One was dark, one blonde, both were tall, fierce, troubled and beautiful. They never spoke publicly of their lives before Catford. It was as if they'd just appeared like magic from nowhere. They had found each other and grown together, working in the theatres on SE6's Great White Way.

Their tales were traced in the memoirs of old thespians, collections of playbills and adverts in local papers. They knocked them dead at the local playhouse and rapidly advanced from the back of the stage to leading roles. Their performances were proclaimed in the *Catford Journal*, *The Stage* and *South London Gazette*. Their film debuts in the early horror picture, *Feast of Blood*, drew more fans even though the film itself was lost when the studio buildings were bombed in 1940.

Raven Bjorn played the wicked sidekick of the film's leading man, Varney the Vampire, and Katherine Ford was the plucky heroine. The film gained them a particular following among the young women of London, the notorious "gut girls" of Deptford, who by day slaughtered animals at Convoy Wharf, but at night adopted the style and sophisticated manners of the woman they referred to as *The* Raven.

Success lured Raven to Hollywood and Katherine, who always wanted proper speaking roles, to the West End. Their exodus from Catford, and the film studio's move to Walthamstow, marked the end of "flapper Catford" and some of the lights on the Broadway were forever dimmed.

Katherine became a huge star, specialising in lovable rogues and bad girls turned good, before she exchanged one form of theatre for another and joined her husband, a Bermondsey doctor, in bringing medical relief to the poor of South London. The local people loved her. To them, she was a true cockney sparrer who had turned her back on fame to help the needy. She brought up her own daughter, Helena, near the Angel pub on the SE16 waterfront.

Helena is my connection to the story. She used to joke with me that one of the two friends got the Queen Mary but her mum got the number 47. It's my bus to work too but I only take it when it's raining heavily or for funerals. Today it is Helena's funeral. That just leaves me to tell the tale.

Imagine getting to know people, scripting their lives, learning about their times and, through a combination of knowledge, skill and research, bringing back magic and recognition, only to see it all vanish again. That's what I do at a lottery-funded project called Breadcrumbs of The Mind – BoTM, or Bottom to staff and our naughtier clients. It's a simple enough concept based on the idea of following a trail of breadcrumbs back home. We encourage older people to block together memories, places and other associations. These are the pathways that, should they succumb to dementia, they, or their loved ones, can use to navigate their way back home. In a sense it's scripting their own life and, given my theatrical background, it suits me.

Objects can be enough to trigger memory and the BoTM project encourages people to engage all the senses – smell, taste, touch and sound as well as sight. One woman I worked with recovered much of her memory after I brought in a space hopper, having seen an old picture of her playing with one. My role is to discover the right key, that elusive shimmer in the grass, a glint in the eye, a half-open door or shining path. Helena, pronounced He lain ah, was a very special shining path, so much so that I sometimes called her the Lady Helena, which seemed to delight and frighten her. I wonder if it helped force a memory.

Helena was elegant, fine boned and funny but also intensely serious. She once showed me a box that, she insisted, was to be buried with her. Inside it was an intricate gold statue of a dancing figure, underneath which was inscribed, in what she assured me was Russian, "To my darling Katerina".

When she showed it to me, I imagined the Raven handing it to the Kat before leaving for Hollywood, an heirloom she'd had engraved as a monument to the friendship between two young actresses determined to succeed. I had fallen a little in love with both Helena and the magic of her mother's relationship with Raven so in my head I quickly projected a parting scene, with variations and costume changes.

I found some information about the Raven and the Kat in old newspapers and uploaded recordings, as well from chatting to Helena. Even though Kat had an accessible back story media-wise, it still pays to dig around and, besides, the incidental stories are brilliant. For example, I'd never heard of the gut girls, a fierce fashion-conscious tribe of women with their own style, a decent wage for a bloody job and a fondness for drinking. For at least one generation of them, Raven and Kat were heroes, style icons and fashion guides. Once, when Raven cut off her hair for a theatre performance, thirty gut girls arrived in the opening week and hurled their own recently shorn locks onto the stage as tribute.

Even when that generation grew up they still followed Raven in Hollywood and eventually it transpired that she was not a fairy-tale princess but a real Russian one who had been hiding her true identity. In 1932, when her car careened off Route One and into the Pacific Ocean, Soviet agents were blamed and in retribution the gut girls burned down the New Cross Communist Party offices. At the Rotherhithe branch, a huge cordon of men, many related to the protesting women, held back the angry mob who had to be satisfied with redecorating the front of the building with blood and guts from the slaughter houses they worked in.

Afterwards, people spoke of Raven as a people's princess. Kat Ford, meanwhile, slipped from the public eye. There is footage on YouTube of a middle-aged Katherine, alongside a young Helena, being interviewed about health in South London. Katherine speaks very clearly in clipped BBC tones. An earlier video features a youthful cockney Kat Ford belting out the music hall classic, *"Knockin 'em Dead on the Barrars of the Walworth Road"*.

Helena once described her mother and Raven as being like Garbo and Barbara Windsor. Gabby cockney versus reserved foreign ingénue. Sometimes she called them Posh and Bexley. As with many of our clients, she occasionally appeared to be confused so when she talked about her mum in the abstract and mixed up the two friends, I put it down to the mental frailty of age.

She once told me, "Kat was the better actress, she loved the role of the doomed princess; but Raven was good at accents and just wanted to be normal."

I thought a lot about this and next time I saw her I questioned her about it and about Raven's gift to her mum of the figurine. Helena looked puzzled and said,

"No, it was always mum's. It's something from our family. *Nash*, as they say in Russian."

It occurred to me that I'd missed something and maybe Helena was actually Raven's daughter, or thought she was. I looked into it and checked some key dates, and I realised that this was impossible.

An alternative was that dementia and confusion had taken hold in Helena's mind. But the rest of her behaviour did not suggest this. At the project we have guidelines about leading people down memory paths or promoting particular versions of events, as the underlying ethos is for people to rediscover and take ownership of their own past and stories. We might nudge them away from delusions that could lead to self-harm, or prompt them to return using the "breadcrumbs" but too blatant a steer is considered counterproductive.

For a few months the talk switched to Helena's own career as a book editor, for a long time at Penguin books on the Strand but also for other companies based around Fleet Street. Many of the breadcrumbs trails I helped devise for her involved the smell of new books and newsprint, and the sounds and sights of routes along the river. We recreated some of her walks to work along the Thames and it was one of these routes that triggered another revelation about her mother.

Helena mostly walked to work from Bermondsey over Tower Bridge and along the north bank but returned home over Southwark Bridge. These areas have changed a great deal since then and the docks have closed but one evening Helena told me something I didn't know. She said that Russian treasures, gold and silver, had once been stored on Tooley Street. The tsarists had originally used the vaults but the Bolsheviks claimed their contents when they came to power. Helena became agitated as she was telling the tale but said that knowing the past enabled her to imagine a different future.

I shouldn't have intervened but I did, asking, "A different future for Raven you mean?"

She stopped and said, "A different future for mum but yes, poor Raven as well. I wish I'd met her, such a brave woman, so full of life. Mum adored her and she never betrayed us, even at the end when she knew the Reds were coming for her."

Helena paused and remembered something.

"Mum got a telegram. I've got it here somewhere, a final farewell just days before the crash."

Helena fumbled in a drawer and pulled out a yellowing piece of paper that had been carefully covered in plastic to protect it.

It read. "My darling Raven. I've not much time. I don't regret my dreams or reaching for them and shall never forget the part you played in realising them. I send you all my love and hope your dreams remain intact and beautiful and, most of all, that you are safe."

It was signed "your Kat".

Suddenly a new scene appeared in my mind-cinema – a flashback, if you like, from the start of the film. In it two shivering teenagers in a badly lit, draughty room south of the Thames shared the secrets of the different dangers they were hiding from. I really felt as if I was there, watching and, even though it was the silent era, hearing the conversation that had "Katherine Ford" saying to Raven:

"Well, why don't you take the name I was going to take? Common old Kat Ford? And," she added with a swish and a flourish, "I can be the mysterious Raven Bjorn. I always wanted to be a princess."

To which came the reply: "I always wanted a normal life. And my real name is Katerina."

Thus the girls switched roles for life. The statue *had* been Kat's all along, the only thing that remained from her Russian childhood.

There were not so very many people at Helena's funeral at Camberwell New Cemetery, just some friends, neighbours and a few theatrical history types. I was the only one there, though, who knew this was the passing of the very last of the Romanovs, my friend the Lady Helena. As I stood in the drizzle of the South London graveyard I thought of another grave, one where one of the best actresses and bravest women of her generation lies. A cockney girl from an orphanage, buried as a foreign starlet and "princess" under a borrowed name in the sun of California.

Sound of the Suburbs

My father was raised in Brixton's Jewish enclave off Effra Road where the doorways to the flatshave mezuzahs on them. My mum's Scottish family roamed the former theatrical digs off nearby Acre Lane. Both were proud of their shift to Beulah and its Hill, which meant they took a dim view of my move to a semi-derelict property in SW8 in the early 1990s. My father saw this as a late outbreak of teenage rebellion at best, but my mother, after a quick comparison of house prices a decade later, did belatedly approve.

My childhood connection to Upper Norwood lives on through football. I still go to the Palace, though I no longer walk to the game down South Norwood Hill from my parents' home. When my own children, Billy and later Laura, were young I created a new family football ritual with them. Together we would take the 196 bus to the match but the return journey would be dictated by the result. If the Palace won we would catch the 196 but in the event of a defeat we returned home by the number 50 to break the pattern of loss. Should the match be drawn, we'd get the train from Thornton Heath (score draw) or Norwood Junction (goalless) to Victoria and then the tube home to Stockwell. Such superstitious behaviour made as much sense as some of the formations that ran out at Selhurst Park and, if nothing else, varied the route to our house near the Larkhall Estate.

My children have left home now but I still sit in the Arthur Waite stand, where to my left the drums and flags of our ultras beat out a consistent rhythm and repertoire of chants. To the right are our guests, driven by the away fan's obsession to make shouty points on another's turf. I enjoy their songs and passions and the way these are refracted through history, form, current narrative and, most obviously, how the game is going.

Very few of our visitors are rude about the Palace as we play in a different league to our former housemates Charlton (1985–1991) and Wimbledon (1991–2003) or would-be rivals Millwall. On our rare meetings, the latter are abusive and refer to our fan base as "the Nigels" but as my name *is* Nigel I don't really feel in a position to complain. At my most recent game the away fans were far too busy attacking their cross-city rivals to be bothered with us though they were roused when an ex-player for those rivals appeared for the Palace. This individual was serenaded with a chorus of "Red and white shite! Hello, hello!"

This ability to rhyme white with shit must be one advantage of being northern, I reflected as I exited the ground, something my children, who both live in the north, may or may not appreciate. Billy is in Preston with his own family and Laura studies in Glasgow, so I travel alone on the number 50 bus to ponder on the game and to rebalance after defeat, for, as Billy once said, being a Palace fan provides one with excellent disappointment management skills.

The number 50 passes through some of South London's lesser known suburbs; once, sitting on the top deck after a defeat in 1998, I had the realisation that very few Londoners live in the city's famous neighbourhoods, whether Chelsea or Knightsbridge, Whitechapel or Peckham. The majority reside in obscure places that most people don't even know exist, never mind have visited. Even fellow south Londoners struggle to recognise Shirley, Furzedown, my own Lark Hall or nearby Springfield, never mind Beulah, Addiscombe or Angell Town. A song from the eighteenth century tried to make sense of all of this:

> *Sutton for good mutton*
> *Cheam for juicy beef*
> *Croydon for a pretty girl*
> *And Mitcham for a thief.*

I had a bicycle stolen in Mitcham when I was fifteen so the rhyme has always made sense to me. I was inspired by Norwood resident Arthur Conan Doyle's Sherlock Holmes to track the miscreant down. Conan Doyle sent his sleuth rattling out into the far south on many occasions and was the catalyst for my own observation that it was in these dozy manors that dreams were made and the assault on Middlesex, and the world, began. Sherlock Holmes described the London Board Schools as "pinpricks of tiny lights" as he gazed out across South London.

My first proper girlfriend was from Croydon, as are Kate Moss, Jamie Reid, Noel Fielding, Kirsty MacColl, Bridget Riley, David Lean, DH Lawrence, Desmond Decker and Jaqueline Du Pre. Or, at least, they lived there once. So did Ronnie Corbett and Ralph McTell, whose *Streets of London* song is an anthem of crushing suburban ambition and potential disappointment if ever I heard one. From further east came David Bowie (Beckenham) and Siouxsie Sioux and the rest of punk's Bromley contingent. My father claims to have met the young David Jones in a greengrocer's in Penge once and seen Billy Idol at a bus stop.

The number 50 plods through Norbury and on down the A23, where well in to the twentieth century it was possible to buy healing water from the Streatham spa and skate, as I did after school, at the International Ice Arena. En route, the 50 could stop to pick up Naomi Campbell, Cynthia Payne or Ken Livingstone in Streatham, which has not always been an extravagantly long red-light district with an intriguingly historic nightclub best known as Caesars.

Caesars was a rite of passage for myself and my friends and, although it was not the first place I kissed a girl, it was the first place I vomited outside of. In 1928, then known as the Locarno, the club was the first purpose-built ballroom in England and closed, as Caesars, eighty years later. This was shortly after it became the country's first lap dancing venue for women, the male strippers treading the same boards as Glenn Miller, Audrey Hepburn, and Charlie Chaplin had once done. It was famous for its violence, both inside and out, and the owner finally bowed to the inevitable and got a boxing venue license. When I went there as a teenager it was rumoured that if the bouncers searched you and found no drugs or weapons they were prepared to provide you with them. Even after its closure and before its eventual conversion to the inevitable luxury apartments, there were rumours that illegal Fight Club style punch-ups went on there.

Just prior to SW18's answer to Manhattan loft-style living, the bus veers off down Poynders Road towards Clapham, via the road named after shy scientist Henry Cavendish. Cavendish discovered hydrogen, or "inflammable air" as he called it, and weighed the world. He weighed the world in *1798*.

When NASA did a "proper" calculation more than 160 years later, using computers and a space view, Mr Cavendish was found to be just 1% out. In honour of this, Billy always sang the man who *weighed* the world and I have this tune in my head as we bounce the final stretch along the Common past the former home of Noel Coward and Billy's old school, Henry Thornton Comprehensive, which is now Lambeth College.

At the other end of Clapham High Street I must decide whether to get off at Union Road or head on to the architectural wonder of Stockwell Bus Garage but there is time to savour another family memory. Laura had been distraught after a particularly unjust defeat to Burnley in December 2001. She sobbed for much of the journey home despite the best efforts of Billy and myself to cheer her up. We finally succeeded in making her smile with a 1970s terrace anthem about a bear. It runs:

> *If you go down to Selhurst Park you're in for a big surprise.*
> *If you go down to the Holmsdale today,*
> *you'll never believe your eyes!*
> *Coz Jeremy the sugar puff bear has bought some boots and cropped his hair,*
> *Today's the day the teddy bears joined the skinheads.*

The song pacified her for a while but when a bunch of moody Chelsea fans got on at Clapham High Street Laura stood up in front of them and gave a full impassioned rendition. They looked at us, burst out laughing and joined in.

One of them pulled out a packet of sweets and another came over to shake my hand.

A third said, "Football eh?"

I recall this event as I step off the number 50. My face reflected in the bus mirror shows no disappointment, only a man who has borne defeat but is secure in who he is, where he is and how he got there.

"Oh South London *is* wonderful," I intone to no one in particular as I stroll down Union Road.

The Commodore of the Pepys Estate

The Raucous green parakeets enlivened the sky over the Pepys Estate then settled in Sayes Court Park. Yusuf Reis welcomed the colourful interlopers as a contrast to the diseased rock doves or chip-fattened seagulls but, like the gulls, they reminded him of different times and other places.

As a retired pirate, Yusuf felt at home on the Pepys Estate as it was practically on the river and notorious for its criminality. His own home stood partly on the old Royal Dockyards, adjacent to Convoys Wharf. This was where British adventurers – Royal Navy or privateer – were once provisioned from. Yusuf sees himself as part of a tradition in Deptford where many in the past, and possibly present, could be described as privateers.

Yusuf enjoyed the history of a place that, in many ways, was where the British Empire was born. He also liked the Rudyard Kipling poem *The River's Tale*, which referred to a time when Yusuf's people first visited the Thames:

While down at Greenwich, for slaves and tin,
The tall Phoenician ships stole in,
And North Sea war-boats, painted and gay,
Flashed like dragon-flies, Erith way;
And Norseman and Negro and Gaul and Greek
Drank with the Britons in Barking Creek,

Not far from Yusuf's flat stood St Nicholas' Church, reached through a gateway flanked by pillars, each of which was topped by a skull and crossbones. On his first visit Yusuf had collapsed into a seat in the graveyard and felt that he really had come home. As many historians had done before him, Yusuf made the connection between the skull and crossbones flag favoured by pirates and the church. The link between privateer and pirate was a matter of perspective; Sir Francis Drake was a privateer to the English, a pirate to the Spanish. In either case, his ships would have been supplied from Deptford.

Other locations had less cheerful associations. River pirates were always hung at Execution Dock in Wapping, where they did what was known as the Marshall's jig. This rictus of death could go on for some time as, unlike other criminals, pirates were choked to death by the noose rather than having their necks broken. After this their bodies were left in the Thames until three tides had covered them.

The mix of celebration and condemnation of his profession in the same city helped Yusuf to develop something that astonished both his fellow exiles and his new London friends. He had always possessed a *good* sense of humour and was an astute observer of the foibles of others. It was only since his arrival in Britain that he truly appreciated, indeed cultivated, the fine sense of duality coupled with surrealism that marked off this most difficult to assume of national traits.

It came to him in stages, but his moment of realisation was at the Albert Embankment after visiting a neighbour at St Thomas' hospital. He was waiting on Lambeth Bridge to catch the C10 home when he saw the sign of the International Maritime Organisation on a building. Yusuf clutched at the bridge wall and laughed so hard that a German couple stopped to ask if he was well.

"As could be expected," he coughed out as he gazed across to the headquarters of the people who had hunted him since he was a teenager. On land, the IMO has no jurisdiction; he could do what he liked. The irony of sharing the same waterfront with the people who had chased him over thousands of miles of ocean, and them being powerless to touch him outside their own headquarters was, he believed, the moment Yusuf acquired a British sense of humour.

Fruit and Nuts

Death was Mandy Jones' first commission. It continued as an uneasy patron over the years via her recreations of Victorian bereavement photographs and a stint at King's Hospital as a mortuary technician and pathology photographer. Mandy never felt it was morbid but wondered if losing her mum when she was quite young was a factor.

Today, Mandy lives with her own family in Kirkdale. She works part-time job in the accounts department of a recycling company and supplements her salary by taking photographs, in particular postcards of the local parks that frame so much of her life. She sells cards for all the seasons but her favourite time is early August, the month her father traditionally declared the opening forage of the year. As children, Mandy and her brother George thought their dad used an astrological chart and imagined he studied the skies and performed spells. In reality, Mr Jones just looked at the weather forecast and organised Mandy, George, their mum plus cousin Sue onto the number 356 bus, armed with buckets, plastic containers and carrier bags.

The early season fruit picking walk began near what is now a Sainsburys and continued along the course of the Pool River towards Kent House. Today this remains South London city as rural idyll, the garden of England re-established alongside the industry, housing and roads. Out-of-control hedges still drip with delicious blackberries, wild apple trees grow and a variety of plum trees (purple, black, yellow or red, depending on the date) are freely available along the pathways, the back of Lower Sydenham Station and on into Cator Park and the allotments beyond.

The Pool is fed by the Beck and the Chaffinch Brook and, near Catford, joins the mighty Ravensbourne, river of ravens, which tumbles through the badlands of Lewisham and Deptford before shouldering its way into the Thames west of Greenwich. The family sometimes met the Beck in Beckenham but rarely went along to Catford, let alone Deptford, because, whilst the walk was charming the food pickings were slim.

As adolescents, Mandy and George mixed and matched the routes to suit themselves, but as youngsters they only ever did the forages in two stages, weeks apart and strictly demarcated. Stage one started as described above and ended at Kent House Road, where they took the 356 home again, laden with fruit to be stewed, jammed, pied, pureed, scoffed and juiced. Stage two involved getting off the bus near Eden Park to plunder the blackberries and raspberries in the fields adjacent to the Bethlehem Hospital, or Bedlam as it is also known.

In the late summer they strolled into the hospital grounds and made free with the apples from trees off the aptly named Monks Orchard Road. George and Mandy sometimes practiced being doctors or nurses. Cousin Sue used to suggest that they'd find it easier passing themselves off as patients and Mrs Jones told them all not to be silly when they described the scrumped crop as "pommes d'insanitee" in an affected French accent.

At school Mandy loved art and worked hard to improve her vocabulary. Her favourite word was "liminal", which she used in the way other people said "bare" or "oh my days" or "sick" as a sort of everyday crutch. She'd describe a positive situation by saying "yeah, it was pretty liminal" or a scary one as "effin liminal" or "he went totally liminal". The forage route is liminal in the proper sense: relating to a transitional stage of a process or occupying a position at, or on both sides of, a threshold that offers exciting, and potentially dangerous journeys.

During the early months of her mother's illness, Mandy and her mum walked some of the paths and talked. After her mother died Mandy walked them alone and continued to ask her mum questions about life that she knew she couldn't answer. It still comforted her to have her mum as a sounding board. Mandy continues to think of the trails as a sort of homage and it could be said that she, George and Sue all grew up along the Pool. All the essentials, such as sex and drugs and rock and roll, came to them there, as did grief and work and achievement and fear.

Drunks and hard youths who considered them terribly posh to be picking fruit were an annoyance, as were dogs and busybodies at allotments who interfered with their raids. There were some places, too, that felt threatening and strange, such as the parallel, fox-babbed and bird-shat path that ran through the woods to Lower Sydenham Station. It was a rich source of fruit and berries but sometimes men sat silently alone on the benches, drinking or reading, half hidden by the foliage. It was as if they were waiting for a train in the wrong place and even though there was precious little to see, George thought they might be bird watchers.

More often accompanied by Sue than George in her teenage years, Mandy kept up the regular hunts in the summer. One time, after their O Levels, they heard music from a unit on the industrial estate. The sound was raw and often stopped while one band member or another got the tune right. The girls sat outside and listened until a few boys from their school came past and disturbed them with crude chat-up techniques. When they failed to make progress the mood of the lads changed and they taunted Mandy, who was very self-consciously flat-chested, about having two backs. At least Sue's ears would provide something to hang on to, they sniggered.

They were still laughing when the music stopped and two huge blokes with rockabilly quiffs slipped out of the rehearsal room for a smoke. Trevor Jones, who was in Mandy's class, broke the silence.

"These your groupies then? Ugly couple. Particularly her with the ears."

At this a smaller lad appeared from behind the original two band members. He was wiry and slight and ginger, and his ears stuck out. He looked at Trevor, then at the rest, and said,

"You want some, do you? Go on, fuck off."

The schoolboys moved off quite briskly and Mandy was about to assert that they could fight their own battles when she noticed Sue and the wiry ginger boy staring at each other as if they'd been hit by lightning. One of the older lads said,

"You girls want to listen to the rest of the set indoors?"

It was a turning point in Sue's life. She shaved the sides of her head, bought checked shirts, sold off all her old records and found her vocation in music promotion and merchandising. For years she toured, travelled and set up deals and itineraries for groups, starting with the one from the industrial estate. Today, Sue lives off the fashionable triangle in Crystal Palace and runs what she insists is a "small" event management company. She had her ears fixed and never settled down with the ginger boy from the band.

"Just as well," she later confided to Mandy. "Kids might have looked like Dumbo."

Mandy didn't lose a cousin to the industrial estate as she and Sue kept in touch, but it could be said that she lost a brother to the fields of Cator Park, where the George she knew went and never quite came back.

George had an ability to focus and research subjects thoroughly. When he was ten years old he did a school project on famous people from Sydenham and ignored John Logie Baird, WG Grace, Ernest Shackleton and Bill Wyman in favour of the music hall entertainer Bud Flanagan. Today it's easy to find out these things with a few clicks on a search engine but back then one had to visit actual libraries and take notes and observe. George transferred these skills to studying nature, especially mushrooms, which the rest of the family appreciated because whilst they all loved to eat them, nobody wanted to be poisoned.

The boon to the dinner table became a danger when George discovered the magical varieties of mushroom and where to find them. Cator Park and Bedlam's grounds had good spots so for him there became two separate hunts; one for belly food, the other for head. The latter opened doors for him and not just doors of perception, as he met new friends and his taste in music changed from the soul and pop of his childhood to electronica and trance. He disappeared for months with what the newspapers dismissively called New Age Travellers, taking his Pool River foraging skills across the country. Mandy once saw him on the news after some trouble in Wiltshire and his infrequent visits home, friends in tow, were often awkward.

Mandy would sometimes suggest they walk the Pool together but George had come to favour drink and chemical recreations, and turned sullen and manic according to whatever narcotic he had taken. There were tense times between their father and George, and when Mr Jones died, George didn't come back for the funeral. After a series of hospitalisations and referrals Mandy recognised that George's trip had taken a seriously bad turn. She was alive to the irony of a foraging trail to a hospital, which led to hallucinogenic drugs, which led to addiction, depression and mental breakdown and incarceration in that same institution. Nowadays her visits to Bedlam are mostly to see George, who is, according to the staff, making progress.

There is a bitter sweetness when Mandy takes her own youngsters to pick fruit every August and, as summer turns to autumn, nuts and mushrooms. She still steals fruit from Bedlam's orchards but no longer refers to them as the apples of madness as that feels too close to home. All her memories of her mum and dad and George and Sue are bound up with the forages, along with a defining moment in her own life.

For her portfolio to support her application to art school, Mandy had chosen to do a photo documentary about the family's foraging route in different seasons, showing the contrast between the industrial and suburban as well as the parks at dawn and dusk. These were places she loved and knew best, and they carried an emotional weight that even as a teenager she recognised as important in a good photograph. If her father was concerned about her visiting the parks, river, footpath and side roads at all hours, he never stopped her.

One dawn, Mandy went to capture the sunrise in Cator Park and found a body slumped on a bench near the river. To her shame, her first thought was that the corpse made an interesting composition. It formed almost a perfect Fibonacci Spiral, cardigan off the shoulder and finger pointing to a tree. The woman was white, in her forties and well dressed, almost as if she was expecting to be photographed, but her face betrayed no expectant joy or smile and her eyes were shut. Mandy took several shots before going in search of help.

The photos aided her college application and she sold several prints, after they had been used in evidence. They were the first pieces she ever sold and some of the others formed the basis of her first exhibition, entitled Strange Fruit and Nuts.

Having a Bubble

I awoke to Cat aggressively shouting his demands for goods and services, specifically breakfast and the opening of windows to enable his morning park inspection. My first thoughts were focused on the previous night's visit to the posh side of my family in Primrose Hill.

My second thoughts concerned what might have been in the gear I had smoked before I got home. I'd escaped from the family early by pleading a morning appointment the next day, then nipped through the fragrant streets of Primrose Hill to the tube and taken the dark shunter south to Kennington where, unlike Chalk Farm, all Northern Line trains ordinarily stop. Except last night they didn't, and the service terminated at London Bridge where I completed my journey on the 133 bus to Newington Butts.

Almost certainly there had been a discussion after I left Primrose Hill that ran:

"Poor Carl. But best not to be too late on those streets."

"Why doesn't he get a taxi?"

"Will they go south at this time?"

"Now, now. Kennington's not so bad. I heard."

"Maybe, but he lives on one of the estates in Walworth. As he says himself, the nearest tube station doesn't always indicate where you live and using a tube name as a means of establishing your locale is just a north London conceit. Mind you – do you say you live in Chalk Farm or Primrose Hill?"

"He lives in Walworth? Really? How brave!" This would be Octavia, the most palatable of the bunch. "I heard it's as rough as a fighting otter down there."

The rest would have smiled at that and the conversation turned to happier topics.

I am not brave or too poor or unable to get a taxi but you judge your evenings by potential outcomes and last night's gathering was definitely no occasion to stay beyond the last tube.

Once back on the sunny side, I strode through what my family no doubt regarded as the mean streets of SE17. There were rough spots, true, but they were easily avoided (or not) and I only went into one of those, the Giraffe pub, because I needed some sanity after the Middlesex yap I'd been listening to for the last few hours.

The Giraffe, or Long Neck as some affectionately called it, was a gin palace with an apothecary sideline. Or a pharmacy that sold beer, if you prefer. The abandoned pool table served chiefly as a flat surface for doing lines on, whilst the cue sticks and balls had all been used up in rumbles over the years. The pub got its name from the fact that, in the long ago and far away, the first giraffe in the UK had been landed at the canal that once ran through what is now Burgess Park. The beast had been allowed to parade about the neighbourhood before being exhibited in the Surrey Zoological Gardens. According to legend, an extension to the back of the pub had been constructed from stones recycled from the old zoo entrance at Manor Place. The zoological gardens had stretched from the site of the council dump and old baths on Manor Place and across Pasley Park. Next door had been the home of Surrey County Cricket Club before it moved to nearby Oval. I loved the idea of men in sportswear with bats ambling through SE17 with the sounds and smells of Asia and Africa and Latin America all around them.

We did have all of that now, but in a different way, and the only wildlife of note were the foxes, cats, pigeons and dogs.

I ordered a cider and looked around for Biffa the herbalist, instinctively moving away from Scrubba and Washa. The former had once been a graffiti artist of some note before spending a few years on the brown, while cider and white had done for Washa's ambitions to be a television presenter, fortified by a cultural studies degree from South Bank Polytechnic. In the British fashion, Washa was so-called because she didn't and Scrubba's name derived from a long forgotten soft drink commercial. It must have been some time ago because I couldn't associate Scrubba with a soft drink of any description.

I found Biffa and bought a few sticks' worth of something he assured me was top quality, to go with my pint. I sipped on one, sparked the other and looked over the premises.

They had all the qualities of an estate pub: multi-racial yet clannish, full of great beauty and tremendously sexy yet unremittingly ugly at the same time, awash with flaring hope and studied despair. At least, that's how my friends from the north might have seen it once they got over the initial shock that the only food being served were nuts and scratchings.

I am an irregular visitor but frequent enough to recognise people at the bar, one of whom, Lily, I knew from my estate. On one memorable evening in the pub she'd distinguished herself by using possibly the last pool cue to batter a bloke who had two-timed her friend Michelle.

"Where you been tonight then?" Lily asked.

"Primrose Hill," I replied.

"What's that like? Any good?" she followed up as she checked out the pub.

"Okay, bit up itself."

"Yeah I heard that. We're off to Dingles later." Their night was only starting.

"I heard that'd been taken over."

And so we drifted into comparisons of the merits and demerits of a selection of local venues before there was an interruption.

Fights escalated fast in the Giraffe and Lily with her native intuition nodded to her confederates, touched my hand and suggested we all exit sharpish. She pulled me through the portal that led out the back way to the rear of George's the newsagents and said, "That was close. It was about to get very lairy in there."

We looked at each other for a while and I was struck just how fantastically turned out Lily and her mates were before I thanked her for the tip-off. Strange smells and sounds greeted me as I turned the corner into Amelia Street. I attributed these to the drains, which often backed up, and the lingering effects of the bob that I had smoked.

I was piecing these reminiscences together as I lay in bed next morning, when I remembered Cat. I put on the kettle, fed the animal and then, tea in hand, wandered to the front room to open the window. I was startled to see that the park opposite appeared to have grown overnight. Across the road was the same attractive arrangement of shrubs and benches but the housing had vanished and instead a sign proudly announced the Royal Surrey Zoological Garden. I fancied that over the top of one of the fences I could see a giraffe. What had been in that gear?

My front room looked the same as always but there was an unfamiliar newspaper lying on the coffee table. It was a stylish thing called Walpaper – The magazine for London's most fashionable borough. The headlines screamed "Lofty Ambitions: Living the High Life Alongside the Canal in the Albany Quarter" and "Walworth

Worthies oppose Fast Food Application on High Street: Local MP Peter Tatchell claims it's out of character for the area". Inside there was a special feature on the celebrity clusters within "Sensational SE17". I was delighted to note that, according to the article, the broadcast media heavyweights favoured Sutherland Square while West Camberwell was the place for the arty mob. Heygate Heights attracted the city types. The literary set could be found between Browning Street and Liverpool Grove, either side of the fashionable souk of East Lane with its parade of designer shops. Stella McCartney had a flat on the canal, Albany Road was filled with people from the music industry and a clutch of film stars lived just south of the zoo between Kennington Common and the Brandon Village.

The phone rang and interrupted my learning about this parallel Walworth. It was Octavia.

"Carl! Oh I'm so glad you're in. I wondered if we could drop by later. I promised the children a trip to the zoo and you know how they love the view from your shared roof."

I muttered something positive.

"They were so excited at seeing Daniel Radcliffe last time."

I said I'd love to see them.

"Oh you are good. You can't imagine how nice it is to get off the hill and into somewhere civilised. There was another stabbing last night on Adelaide Road, it's the third this month. And Alfred couldn't get a taxi from the West End last week unless the driver was paid in advance."

"That is shocking," I said and without thinking about it added, "Shall I meet you at the tube and we could go in the zoo that way?"

"I thought we'd get the 133 from the river and meet you at Butts Park? The children love the journey around the Elephant, it's all so elegant. Oh, and could we go to the canal later? You're so lucky living in a beautiful part of the city."

I concurred and from my window eyed what looked like a rather elegant café next to the railway, which in my memory had been home to an ugly training centre for the unemployable. Let them serve cake, I mused, or buns for the elephants.

On the way through Newington to meet Octavia, I met coffee fair-trader Biffah returning from his jog and noticed E'Screwbar and Wah Shah strolling arm in arm.

Biffah grinned and said, "I'd avoid those two if I were you. He's been offered half a million for his next book and she's going to be on the Late Cultural Review as co-presenter. Ran into them at Cou Long last night, couldn't get away. They nattered on and on about a north city cultural tour they'd just been on. You'd think it was Beirut the way they kept going. I mean it can't be that bad, can it? You've family there after all."

I nodded and he continued.

"They'd been up at the site of Watkin's Tower. Apparently the rebuild is way over budget but one thing they did tell me that was quite funny was that there used to be a zoo up in NW1. Nearly as popular as ours but when the royal family shifted the animals from the Tower of London they gave them to us along with a subsidy and that tipped the balance. The other zoo closed and the area sank into poverty."

Night time

Bank Holiday Weekend

The rain shuddered down and the wind blasted through the estates south of Camberwell. Tony glanced from his window at the top end of Ruskin Park, its trees buffeted by the gale and the passing number 468s streamed with moisture. There was clearly no point going out in those conditions.

Further west, in Clapham, the stallholders at the Country Affair stared ruefully at the sky. One of them paused and said, "You know what the Cockney shepherd said, don't you? 'Red sky at night, Camden's alight'."

No one laughed, although a couple of veterans of this franchised festival of country arts did wonder whether it hadn't been tempting fate (or fête) to opt for this event rather than the more traditional Lambeth Country Show at Brockwell Park in July.

"Even if the weather had been good, I'm not sure how many people would have paid to come to this," said one of the sheepshearers. "It's free in Brixton and you get dub reggae."

"Better organic home-grown, too," replied the man who ran the owl sideshow, looking around him. "But this is Claahm. More money than sense round here now."

The monied folk of Clapham, like the rest of the city, had enough sense to stay indoors. Not even the prospect of lamb barbering, pig barbeques and being photographed with the genuine 'edwig aht of 'arry Potter was tempting them out. Elsewhere, although owls had never been on the menu, millions of people readjusted their plans in the face of the gloomy weather. In actual fact, that was half the problem – most people hadn't made any plans, so there were none for them to adjust. Lulled by a sunny April and a hot few days in the run-up to the spring bank holiday, significant numbers had thought they would just be able to pitch up in the parks, along the river, in friends' gardens, and snooze away the weekend pleasantly.

Instead, as the temperature dropped into the low end of single figures, winter parkas were donned in what in other circumstances might have been regarded as a retro gesture involving the possibility of scrapping with greasers in Southend or Brighton. Ground frost was reported in the north and, while the temperature never fell that low in the metropolis, summer wardrobes that had been worn since the end of March were quietly put to one side, along with the swimsuits ready for the opening of Tooting Bec Lido. By five o clock on Saturday afternoon sales of soup had taken an unexpected upturn.

Art galleries and other indoor attractions experienced a huge surge in demand, so much so that the Horniman Museum had to provide extra sheltered parking spaces for buggies and prams as the city career-break mums of south London's various nappy vales and valleys descended en masse. In the café, the word "wholemeal" had been carefully covered up on the sandwich menu because, since lunchtime, staff had been running to the local corner shop to buy up stocks of what the Germans in their wisdom call simply *toastbrot*. Extra staff had been brought in to help as a result of the unexpected boom in interest in stuffed mammals of dubious authenticity and themed anthropological exhibits.

It was clear that not everyone was having a terrible time; but everyone Tony knew was. As he finished the fifth in a series of dismal phone calls to or from various chums, he turned to his flatmate Shawnee and said, "Do you know, I've half a mind to call the Samaritans".

Shawnee, who was recovering from a summer cold and reading a book, looked up. As a child she'd spent her summer holidays in Barmouth, mid-Wales and was therefore quite inured to the disappointing juxtaposition of the words "holiday" and "violent freezing squall".

"Things aren't that bad, surely? I thought you were looking forward to a rest and this does rather give you the opportunity."

"I wasn't thinking about calling them for help. I'm just curious about how many more calls they get on a weekend like this." He lit a cigarette, inhaled, and continued. "Everyone I've spoken to is running a blue, no one wants to do anything or be bothered much about going out. I mean, I hadn't planned much, just thought I'd sit in the park chatting."

"That's it, you see," she said. "If you had planned something, then you'd get on with it but, as it is, you're just adrift. Could be worse, though. If you were still going out with laughing girl from South Croydon you'd have spent half the weekend on the number 468 and the rest in some underground art happening space. Or whatever."

"Or whatever. There is that, I suppose," Tony echoed. "She never was much of a one for the sun, though. Nor was her mate Hexie. Odd coincidence – Hexie broke up with her partner at the same time we did." There was a slight pause, as if he had more to add, but a trilling sound interrupted him. "Ahh. The phone again."

Similar tableaux were being enacted throughout the zones, hidden villages and clustered communities of London. By Sunday evening, even those who had set out on trips to the countryside began to return early with tales of swollen rivers, battered campsites, seafronts where the rain had whipped discarded chips into lard, festivals reduced to sandal-strewn wastelands and a series of complaints and agues not heard of at Whitsun since the Middle Ages. Sales of vitamins, wellingtons and whisky hit summer peaks, while stocks of Pimms were shuffled gently but swiftly to the back of stores like an incontinent relative in a wedding photo.

More than forty stops south, as the number 468 flies, a woman was sauntering along breezily, moving strongly against this downbeat trend. She was pretty, in a sharp-featured way, and wore calf-length boots, black and white striped tights, a dark skirt mostly covered by an eye-catching red mackintosh, and a red rubber rain-hat from which her dark hair just crept out. The breeze was at her back, as in the Irish blessing, though she was happy not to have the sun in her face. She skipped through the puddles, past the scowling faces of other pedestrians.

She slowed up to watch a jack-knifed lorry that had become trapped after skidding on the flooded roadway. Opposite, some pub awnings were doing their best to be cheery with jaunty colours and pots while below them the punters stared out glumly. As the woman crossed the pavement, she loosened one of the notches in the belt of her mac and briefly began to whistle a low, haunting tune with a folksy feel. The wind began to rise. She ducked as a ripped umbrella from a pub garden flew past her head and embedded itself in a hedge. Laughing, she crossed the Brighton Road and bounced up to a shabby black door just a few doors along from the Swan and Sugar Loaf. Here she stopped and rang the buzzer.

The door opened and she flew up the stairs to the third floor, dislodging a broom on the landing as she entered the flat. Once inside, she carefully removed her rain things and stooped to pick up a charcoal coloured cat that had entwined itself around her legs. A woman's voice came from the other room.

"Put the kettle on, would you? I'll be done in a minute." Then, after a brief pause, "Hey, were you whistling just now? Pretty impressive, if you were. At least four pub umbrellas took off and one of those annoying giant plastic beer bottles flew into a 468."

"Really? How funny. Earl Grey or British Rail?"

"Oh, builders, I think. There are some Tunnock's Tea Cakes in the cupboard."

Pushing aside a series of strange packets, she pulled down the bright red and yellow box, just as a short, curvy woman appeared at the door. She had long, curly brown hair and mischievous eyes, which, unfortunately, were often overlooked in favour of her pronounced chin and the wart at the end of it. Smiling, she took the cup of tea and said, "Thanks, Red Cap. Good to see you. Thirsty work that, you know. I've been spinning all weekend. But it all seems to have come off alright, doesn't it? What had your guy been planning?"

"Oh I think a bike ride and then lounging about the park in the sun, meeting with his wanky Peckham mates. And yours?"

"Barbeque Saturday, Greenwich market today and I believe there was talk of a jaunt to Brockwell Lido if the weather was right for tomorrow."

"Well done, Hexie! I suppose we should carry on, then. I mean, it wouldn't do for them to get any hopes up at this late stage. Shall I take up the thread?"

So the happy pair continued industriously spinning away, whistling and loosening knots in Croydon.

Nearer the Thames, Tony sat dejected.

"It's not like there's anything on TV, even. They must figure everyone will be out doing things."

That, of course, was not what anyone was doing, and all the favoured outdoor haunts of the bank-holidaying Londoner remained desolate. No hordes sprawled out in Dulwich Park; walking tours didn't dawdle along Bankside's famous Elizabethan red light area; the South Bank itself was as free of tourists as Kennington Park was of Latin American families; outside the Vauxhall Tavern, only a few on stronger pills shivered on the old pleasure grounds; Battersea Park was blissfully untroubled by Aussie rules or Frisbee golf.

Tony was absent-mindedly watching the news reports of a truly wet and lost weekend when Shawnee, who had now finished her book, asked, "You don't regret ending it do you?"

"No, not at all. Fucking witch."

Sung by the Neck

Old Shad Thames is flowing where the watercress grows,
Where my heart is I am going to my one wild rose.
The moment I meet her with a hug and kiss I'll greet her,
There's not a sort sweeter where the Shad Thames flows.

"Ohhh golden tonsils!"

The woman toys with her hair but keeps her other hand firmly on the small boy next to her. So tightly that he complains.

A tall, dark-skinned woman next to her points to the singer and addresses her friend: "He's properly hench, isn't he Amy?"

"Fit as, Sashley, fit as." Amy is shorter, curvier, blonder and definitely interested. "Not too old for me, I think."

"My mum saw him at Bermondsey the other day," adds a fit-looking Latina woman on a pause between cleaning jobs at the leisure centre and the so-called Gillette Tower.

"My gran watched him playing that new square behind the Elephant," Sashley says and, glancing at Amy, continues, "I saw him first."

"Maybe," says Amy," but he saw me!"

I can hear both Sashley and Amy and I see them both, but I wish to add that I am admired in more locations than that, from Mary Harmsworth Park to Shad Thames.

It is only natural that, as so many people have done before them, they squabble over me. Because I am beautiful or, if you prefer, comely, bonny, dapper or ravishing. My height gives me a regal air, my red hair cascades past my shoulders and the sun never fails to pick up the green tint to my eyes. I have a smooth way of moving. It looks languid and slow but in reality it is very fast. I'm closer than you think and I have hidden depths. My smile stops children's tears and weakens women's resolve, my friendly face indicates a cheery manner and relaxed demeanour. I am elegant, stylish and musical, at my best with the guitar. Songs flow from me, sweet, bitter, happy and melancholy.

In the bleak squares along the New Kent Road my haunting compositions about empty watery spaces and rural scenery are well received. People marvel at how I deliver the ancient songs of the Surrey countryside to the modern city. No one believes me, or they assume I am being pretentious, when I tell the truth and say that I am the ancient songs of the landscape. I can be pretentious, but not about that. I just don't tell them the whole truth, which is that I am a shapeshifter, a waterhorse. Or, as the Saxons called me, and after all they named most things around here, I am a neck, a necker or, to their Scandanavian cousins, Nix. I traditionally appear as human or horse as fancy takes me but again, even if I did tell people this, they wouldn't believe me. They'd laugh at the idea that I sometimes take people away, make them disappear, I'm far too charming to be suspected of something like that.

So it is only natural that I knew the landscape that existed before this one and the one before that and the one before that. Most especially, I know my river that rises near St Georges' Cathedral and enters the Thames just East of Tower Bridge. It is all in my DNA and, although there are new place names to learn, they nestle between the old ones. This land was familiar to me even before the Saxons' new settlement (Newington) and south of it the farm of the Britons (Walworth) and the two areas north, the place where the cattle were landed (Rotherhithe) and the island belonging to Beormund (Bermondsey). Centuries pass and fashions change but I've always ploughed the fields for all the ladies in all the ends around here over time.

One of my art student fans once called me a method performer but I am much more than that. They use words like authentic and credible, and frequently cite my performances on their mobile networks.

I give them my nom de guerre, the name I perform under, Nicks Bäckahäst, but add casually, with a smile and slow eye fluttering, "You can call me Nix". I know that the students will spread the word on What'sChat and SnapApp.

St Mary's Newington Churchyard

I met my love at the Gallows dock,
Mill cranes and bodies sway.
And oh, the love I felt was a shock
Words could never say.
Took her sailing up my river,
Bermondsey was mine to give her.

Many of my regulars frequent the old Newington churchyard but are outnumbered by casual attendees, bystanders and people stopping between errands. Camp followers aside, there are distinct variations in the crowds, depending on my chosen performance spots. At Mary Harmsworth Park and Paragon Gardens there are more grey hairs, whilst Newington and Elephant Square are full of working women, the shiftless poor and students. The latter's needs, longings and weaknesses excite me, as do the many new arrivals from the southern Americas. In Bermondsey there are more men in the parks while Shad Thames swarms with out-of-town visitors and various breeds of scriveners.

I scent desperation, deprivation and deficiency and they smell release in me, they spy hope, kindred otherness and an externalised charm that they identify in themselves. I feed off their need and graze on their damaged beauty but I have my favourites, the tall, dark-skinned woman and her plumper blonde friend being two of them. Several of the mums straying away from their children by the swings and the office ladies stopping by at lunchtime in their well-cut garments are also untroubling to my eye and, I think, desirous of my embrace.

Some make requests for their favoured tunes and the pleasure is all mine in granting their fancies.

Elephant Road

There was an old woman and she lived in the castle Weela Weela Walyer.

There was an old woman and she lived in Walworth, down by the river Neckinger.

She had a baby three months old Weela Weela Walyer.

She had a baby three months old down by the river Neckinger.

She had a penknife long and sharp Weela Weela Walyer,

She had a penknife long and sharp, down by the river Neckinger.

She stuck the penknife in the baby's heart Weela Weela Walyer,

She stuck the penknife in the baby's heart, down by the river Neckinger.

The square is brash and lacks the intimacy of the old Heygate woods in which I once ensnared light-foot maidens. Today the people are more coiffured but single women with children, and the use of knives, are very much part of Walworth's present and past. Who can forget Alice Diamond and her Forty Elephants gang? Or the Edwardian boys with their razors and sharpened combs?

People like it when I connect with the past; the elderly remember, and the youngsters feel they are part of something. Old ladies moisten at the sight of me, young mums pine for freedom, the studious become giddy with yearning and the already overheated lust for me to lift them up to a more exalted place or, at least, a more private one. I savour their passions and hear their excited chatter. They are enthralled by me. There is even a fan group of which, I'm happy to note, blonde Amy and dark Sashley are members.

Sashley in her branded urban threads breaks all laws of residency, class and custom by mixing with the students in their denim and dreads. Not for her the mutual suspicion of yard and shard and, at her lead and, I think, my inspiration, others from the neighbourhood chat openly with the freelancers and artists from Oldham and the Orient, Columbian restaurant workers share a joke with Caribbean council employees.

I am a river to many peoples, as the old saying goes.

Paragon Gardens

The arms of a Bricklayer I gave her there,
as a ribbon for her hair.
From New Kent Road to the Elephant,
cheek to cheek we stomped.
Her necklace made of the A2 overpass,
her loveliness was unsurpassed.
Kissed her again at Walworth Road,
it made our desires explode, Sweet Necker.

Occasional passing cyclists join the locals in this green afterthought and dog toilet alongside an urban clearway. The traffic swishes by on the New Kent Road but I cannot neglect my course or disappoint my adoring public. The residents near the Paragon do not get much entertainment or a chance to tell their stories. I bring both, as some of "my" students interview them for a "performance project" about the area. Based around my performances obviously.

The pensioners speak of the Grand Surrey Canal, which I remember well, and further back still to the great Walworth marsh, into and out of which three rivers flowed and drained. Birds of all kinds made their homes on the wetlands, and along the banks of the Neckinger, Effra and Earl's Sluice, while otters and beavers hunted in the bountiful eel-filled waters.

I sing canal shanties and marsh ballads, and I sing of the birds, the screaming jay, the booming bittern, the joyous call of the thrush and liquid warble of the blackbird. I conjure up the great feathered armies that flew behind the plough. My audience soars and glides up and away, transported by my exquisite vocals, carrying the memories of flight, feather and fur. It is hard to know the extent to which I've reached the beautiful Sashley. She's interested in my fine limbs and full lips but is far too detached for my liking. Her blonde friend Amy would come with me tomorrow, of that I am certain.

Tabard Gardens

At Spa Gardens I held her hand,
At Jamaica Road I faced her.
At the Tabard Park I kissed her mouth,
And tenderly embraced her.
Heard the bells of St Mary's ringing,
All the time, my heart was singing.

The Tabard Gardens audience are a young, tough crowd, full of rage, sap and urges, not to mention furious disappointments. Many have a strong sense of injustice and quite a number have been incarcerated themselves, but no one does loss and yearning the way I do. No one else has the practice or experience. I know my audiences and I speak to them, to their hearts and, even if they don't know it, their psyche, as I time travel through all the local jails; the Marshalsea, the Horsemonger, Kings Bench, Clink, as well as the dreadful events at the police lock-ups in Bermondsey and Carter Street. Enforced separation by prison, exile or employment runs deep with people here, they are in a sense transient and I sing of eternity, I sing of place and belonging to it.

As I belt out the sonnets of jail, crime, hurt and injustice I spot plump Amy lolling with a group of friends but no Sashley. Where can she be? Has she something more important to do? She must be ill.

St Mary Magdalen Churchyard

If I dip into your water,
Fall through my reflection.
I will shadow myself anyway,
Have you ever seen my face?
Fast asleep and dreaming?
And it don't feel right,
That I don't get no sleep at night.

Sashley is back; I can see her looking me up and down, oh the things I'll do to that minx with her wide red mouth and her slim limbs. She lends gusto to my songs of worship and religion, of the eternal and redemption, of sin, lust and punishment. Religion is wasted on the virtuous, it is so much more compelling to consider from the other angle. She inspires me to consider new things, seize fresh opportunities and dream of bigger possibilities in life and music.

Sashley is the muse but a "duck" helps the idea take shape. One such "duck" trundles past my source as I rest. It is part bus and part boat, with the word "Tours" written on the side. I follow it to the Thames and it glides into the water with people on board. No one complains and I think to myself, if a such a crude thing can take so many people to the water then I, as a waterhorse, should have no trouble "scaling up" as I believe people say.

I am cunning and set about my plotting. I eavesdrop conversations, insinuate my way into groups and thus learn the best night and the best time to involve the most people. Then, fox-like, I set to work on what I have learned is called "promotion". My tongue has never been more silver, my words never smoother. A special concert at a secret venue is the lure and I promise a personal appearance after the show. I have arranged the transport; I am the transport.

As a horse I can carry two people at most, but as a bus, they can all get on board, even if I am only a single decker. I make certain my two particular friends will be available on the night.

Tanner Street Park, or Leathermarket Gardens

> *Sweet Neckinger flow softly,*
> *made Jacob's Island into a crown.*
> *Flow sweet river, flow,*
> *made a brooch of Tanner's town.*

Some very well turned out men and boys in Bermondsey follow me with eyes that burn and lips that yearn. The area is no longer exclusively porter and scullery class but they are still muscle clad. Leathermarket is where my nurses come, trim in their uniforms, so healthy and so fragrant. They contrast with the past when this district stank of drains, cattle flesh, dog waste and urine from the tanneries and processing works. My river that once bubbled freely through the fields was filled with filth and poison, in effect murdered, and carried a lethal cocktail onwards into the Thames. I conjure up that almighty reek and roar my songs of industry, of dirty old towns, of factories and poverty, or I chirrup of dead birds, fishes, trees and destruction of the hop fields. I am loved by the environmentalists who tidy the gardens and tend the allotments because of these songs, but it is not pious fury or a romantic idyll I'm conjuring. I mean it, I lived through and witnessed those evil times, and the devastation twisted my naturally sweet disposition, just as the effluence poisoned my course.

The songs of industry cause me to wonder whether Sashley works. Men's attentions spoil Amy but she spends some time at a counter, selling perfumes and ointments. Sashley must get coin from somewhere and I think not on her back, and neither is she from a noble family. I should pay closer attention to her but that would conflict with the many other attractive demands on my time. Besides I'll have plenty of time to find out anything I want after the "bus" trip.

Shad Thames in the daytime

> *Oh Shad Thames I might be dreaming,*
> *The stars fell down on the factory.*
> *The cathedrals repeating, the light receding.*
> *Have you ever seen my face fast asleep and dreaming?*
> *Oh Shad Thames, the lightning fell.*

There is an army for me at the riverside. A seething mass of people. Some of them have come especially, others drawn by curiosity about what the commotion is. The glow of my presence shines down equally on tourists, office workers, my beloved acolytes and hangers on, who all sing, sway and dance to my call. My mind reels with their applause and the memory of previous crowds that once came to see me perform where my river meets the Thames, to see pirates jig their gallows dance and hear my ballads of murder and the New World of monsters and brigands of treasure and loss. The memory brings with it the sweet tang of cholera and unscrubbed skivvy thighs, of dead babies and drunks falling off the rickety planks of multiple drownings in the holes, trips and ponds of the island of Jacob.

I think then of my evening plans and I sing with joy and anticipation in a way I haven't done for many years.

Shad Thames after dark

I pick up my congregation, as well as a couple of extra passengers who mistake me for a real bus, from the so-called "Hellraiser" stop on the Old Kent Road. I've promised a unique event for the evening at a venue no one has seen before. I hear the excited chatter, arguments and speculation all the way up to the final moment where we trip off Jamaica Road and down into the depths of St Saviour's Dock, deeper than anyone thought possible, down into the darkness, into the depths of the old river, into my lair, my cave, my home. No bird sings here, no phone calls out and, to my disappointment, no Sashley on board. The discourteous vixen.

My decision is quick, lordly and merciful, though sparked by anger at her impertinent failure to show. I have to recognise that it is her I crave and I am vexed at her insolent refusal to recognise what an honour that is. Any of the others, including lush buxom Amy, would gladly sacrifice anything to my majestic whim. As it is, I have to leave the rest of them suspended between life and death underground as I slip off my bus disguise, take Amy's phone and rise to the surface to make the call.

I make a song, if not dance, of it.

> *Sashley if you want to release your friends*
> *And have them returned to their ends.*
> *Greet me by my proper name or give yourself to me*
> *You have two moonrises and name guesses three.*
> *You could text to make your answer easy.*

The title is *Ransom Song* and it appears as a video message on the What'sChat group.

Rockingham Estate, SE1

In a third floor flat in Whitworth House, Sashley is watching the video with her gran, who is the reason she missed the bus. No one else had been available to take the old lady home from an appointment at Guy's Hospital and sit with her afterwards. The message plays three times before disappearing. Sashley quickly puts out the word that no one else in the group, who missed the trip, is to try guessing and waste the three opportunities. She stares at the screen.

Her Gran asks, "Are you saying he kidnapped a whole bus full of people?"

"Apparently. But how do you hide a bus? Even a red one in London?" Sashley replies.

"Maybe it's a magic bus or not even a bus at all? You remember when you were little and you liked fairy stories? How there were these places right next to our world but totally separate, like a parallel universe."

"Like the book with the girl and the white bear? Dark Materials, quantum something?"

"Yes, or what if he's like in Doctor Who and gone through some portal? Then there's no way they'd find it or the people is there?"

"He's not a timelord! He's just a fit busker, gran!" .

"I've something to show you. When I saw him at Elephant Square that time, it triggered a memory."

Her gran pulls out a blue plastic wallet about four inches square, inside of which are photographs back to back so you can flick through them. There are twenty in all and many of the pictures feature the same two young women.

"Gran! Who told you that tank top was a good idea with your tits!"

"That's me and my friend Mary."

"What's with the horses?"

"They used to pull the barges sometimes, carry stuff to East Lane. Mary was obsessed with them, she used to say that one day she'd ride away on one. Thing is, I think she did."

"Wait – what's he doing there?" Sashley stops and opened the photo album wider towards her gran.

"Looks the same, doesn't he? Except for the flares."

"He'd be, what? Your age by now, wouldn't he?"

Her gran nods. "I didn't make the connection at first, I mean my memory isn't what it was but then I found these. I remember Mary saying how she was going out one night for a ride, I thought she was being filthy but now I think she meant it literally. There was this particularly lovely horse that she used to feed and I think she vanished on it."

"Like the bus?"

"Like the bus. Sashley. You have to think about what he is really. Where he lives. Here."

Her gran touches her heart and Sashley screams, "I don't know what he is really! Do you? Does even he?"

Her gran holds her face and stares at her. "Think about what I tell you. Always, we live in our heart, what we are. Think: what is he to you? What does he have to do? Whatever he is, what does he do?"

"He sings. He sings in the same places. Can you let go of my face, it's hurting."

"To knock some sense into you. He sings. That is what he does. We all know this and we know where. So that is how we find him."

Sashley shares the plan with the others in the fan group, the ones who didn't make it to the bus. The next night they split up and each person covers a different busking point. Sashley approaches her spot from Archie Street, styling, as she imagines, a ninja look, and hides in a dark corner as the sounds of the night-time city settle around her.

Across Tanner Street Park, near the children's play areas, sits a familiar figure. Beautiful, alone, sad and forlorn, he sings.

Where by the marshes flies the nightjar
Neckar the soulless one sits with his guitar
Sits inconsolable, friendless and foeless
Waiting his destiny – Neckar the soulless

In the bushes Sashley waits till he has finished, then texts a name to the others. The name she texts is Neckar. His name is Neckar.

Then she quietly leaves him to his eternity of loneliness.

Keep Smiling Through

1980s

Pete: Miles away in Brixton, at the other end of the 196 bus route, the city burned in the summertime, and across the north of England whole towns existed on stewed cabbage and domestic pets. At least, that's how we understood the news. No one we knew was on the dole, other than by choice, and it seemed the poorer you were the better your football team.

Mark: I was fifteen before I saw a London side win the league and even then it was the Arsenal, who, as traitors to the Woolwich, don't count.

Pete: Palace were the fashionable club, with memories fresh from the Malcolm Allison and Terry Venables eras. Other lads were drawn to the crazy antics at Plough Lane or the atavistic violence of the Den. There were also the poor saps, as we saw them, doomed by family tradition to support the fallen aristocrats of Charlton Athletic.

Mark: Refugees from other parts of London brought with them strange allegiances to West Ham, Tottenham and even QPR but Chelsea were an abomination, rapidly establishing a reputation for rubbish football on the pitch and violence off it.

Together: This didn't fully explain the Smilers.

Pete: We weren't sure then what the Smilers did, exactly, except that they were to be feared and avoided.

Mark: Older children talked of them touring the area in a transit van, accosting kids and offering them ciggies or sweets before drawing them into a conversation about football.

Pete: Others described a quiz designed to test one's knowledge of, respect for, or support of, the Pensioners. Adults, when they thought no children were listening, spoke of "fiddling", which caused me to wonder whether the Chelsea Smilers were a musical group.

Mark: There were whispered tales of murdered children found abandoned on the railway lines and waste grounds that mark the great southern wen. Whatever they were, they inspired terror across south London and the county borders, and the police seemed powerless to stop them.

Pete: Ordinary kids had been, in my gran's words, interfered with. She said that the Smilers sometimes didn't kill them but turned kids into one of them.

Together: We assumed this meant a Chelsea fan and were suitably appalled. Sometimes, people forgot about them for months but barely a summer went by when there wasn't at least one Smiler scare.

Pete: Mark and I were best friends and neighbours. We walked to and from school together. We were Clough and Taylor or George and Andrew, depending on what we were talking about, and that day it was football.

Mark: Pete and I were best friends and neighbours. We walked to and from school together. We were Clough and Taylor or George and Andrew, depending on what we were talking about, and that day it was football.

Together: The coach had kept us back so we walked home later than usual and the leaf-blown late September streets were quieter, without the excited jabber of an exiting school.

Mark: Too quiet. I caught a glimpse of movement as we rounded the corner into the avenue.

Pete: A blue transit had taken the corner past the Video Cabin just a bit too swiftly, and tore towards us.

Together: We exchanged worried glances.

Mark: Seconds later, the doors flew open and we were surrounded. Four blokes wearing jeans and green shiny jackets, and the thing I noticed was that they were blokes, not lads.

Pete: They sported fighting stubble and were tooth-missing veterans of the golden age of football violence. Addressing Mark, one of them said:

"You alright, mate? You look lost."

Another joined in. "Looks nervous to me. Looks like he's something to hide. Odd colouring, might be part silver."

A third, taller and better dressed than the others, said softly, "Well. What of it?"

Mark: This was a life-defining moment and I wasn't ready. I've wept about it since, wished to have the time again. I was unprepared and my true character was revealed.

Pete: Mark stepped away from me and pushed me towards them. He said,

Together: "It's him you want! He's Millwall and he's part Irish."

Mark: I fled and felt a boot on my thigh. I saw the taller one holding Pete and the van's doors open then close again.

Pete: With that he fled and the taller one held onto me then he shoved me through the open doors.

Together: The van sped off past the school.

Mark: I sat down, stared at the road and wept. A skinny student, one we teased because his name was David Round, who lived in the big house on the avenue, approached. He had a bottle of wine in his hand and he shared it with my distraught mum after he walked me home.

Pete's mum withered in front of me. Her lovely auburn hair turned grey overnight. It was dreadful to see her watching all day from her window. Shame burned me. She didn't know what I'd done, but I did.

My parents played it well. It can't have been easy for them to move at their time of life, yet all the focus was on me and how I coped in a new school. They pretended that they were moving for reasons of their own but really it was all about me from the off.

21st century

Mark: I've not been down our old street, near Hermitage Road, since the end of the miners' strike.

Pete: Mark hadn't walked those streets for twenty years. Until today.

Mark: I took the 196 from Stockwell Green to deliver a report into the drugs economy in south London.

Pete: Mr Round's former residence had been turned into a cannabis factory. The police had asked the media to cover it as part of a story about successful raids across the capital and Surrey.

Mark: I delivered my report to camera then slipped off into the old neighbourhood. I stopped outside "our" house and some Ghanaian kids stared suspiciously at me. Then I heard a voice coming from a space between my old house and Pete's.

"You alright mate? You lost?"

It was a child's voice but it sounded as if its throat was blocked.

Pete: No one found my body.

Mark: The face was corroded but the eyes were still recognisable, as was the sandy hair. The mouth was unnaturally wide with two cuts either side.

Pete: Well, well. It's been time. It really has been time.

Mark: Pete?

Pete: Nice life you made for yourself, talking. People trust you, don't they? The famous reporter.

Mark: Pete?

Pete: Seen you on the telly. Other people's, obviously. Don't have my own and, anyway, not really equipped to switch channels am I?

Mark: You're not real.

Pete: What – just light and words? Like you? Public figure, standing up to criminals, boldly calling out bullies. You must have grown into the role. I never got the chance, did I?

Mark: You can't be real.

Pete: You know they really do wedge a card in your mouth and punch, making the sides of your face split. After everything else, as an afterthought.

Mark: I'm really sorry. I never meant... I was just a kid.

Pete: My mum died in this house. I saw her when I came back. She didn't see the changed me. I wasn't Millwall anymore. But then, I never was, really, was I? And I never used to smile like this did I?

****

His mouth widened until it almost reached his ears and Mark screamed and screamed and screamed.

So did Pete.

A Gold for Big Ben

"Are you the boxing fellow?"

She bobbed her head in a fashion that was both assertive and placatory. It was also, in the sport I commented on, sometimes the precursor to an overhand right. I discounted the chances of her landing a blow on me but there was a bit of the fighter's duck-and-weave about her movements.

The area around the hill with five names – Denmark, Herne, Red Post, Champion and Dog Kennel – specialised in such formidable women. Pilates-trained strong central core, fit from summers swimming at the lido and walking up from the Herne Hill shops with produce. She also had that polite but persistent tone that came from being in late middle age and not caring, too much, what others thought.

People often approached me in this fashion but normally they were larger, younger, frequently darker, nearly always more masculine and never while I was relaxing in the reading garden of the Carnegie Library. I had learned, however, from coverage of the sport, and living in south London, never to judge people on grounds of build, race, age, gender or venue when it came to the potential for a rumble.

"I write about pygmachia, yes." I used the Greek word to show her that I was not about to be intimidated by a retired schoolteacher type. "How may I help you?"

She rolled with the implied rebuke and asked, "Have you ever heard of a boxer called Ben Caunt?"

"Big Ben Caunt? The one the tower's named after?"

"Technically it's just the clock face," she wrinkled her nose to make it clear that she didn't hold my ignorance against me, "but yes, that Ben Caunt."

"The one with the strong and durable, yet also slow and clumsy style?"

"I've no idea about his style. Would you like to interview him?"

"The Torkard Giant who was born over two hundred years ago? You want me to interview a dead boxer? Lady I'm used to boxers whose careers have corpsed. Boxers who are stiffs in the ring. But I draw the line when they stop breathing. I find it inhibits two-way communication."

82

"I don't know when he was born but I can vouch for his presence and availability for interview now." She softened. "For you or me, yes, of course, it's impossible, but my friend Becca is a medium and she gets all sorts from the other side. This boxer chappie started coming through strongly. He's got something important to say but, my dear, I think he needs to tell someone who'll understand and, sympathetic though Becca and her circle are, they're no boxing experts."

This was the classic (mental) bolo punch, relying on surprise and odd angle of approach rather than force. In a career spanning some decades I had never had the opportunity to interview a Victorian prize fighter. At the very least this meant I could settle the question of whether the clock was named after him and clear up some other matters about Ben Caunt's rather mixed career. By his own reckoning he'd been the first world heavyweight champ, and English champion several times, only to have the title removed due to dirty fighting. As his last fight had been more than a decade before the Marquess of Queensbury brought in rules for boxing, the mind boggled at the earth-shattering act of aggression that might have constituted "dirty fighting" in his day.

Not wishing to be laid out by a sucker punch, I parried, "So, you'll have to forgive me here. I'm a little unclear as to the protocol involved in interviewing the deceased. What is the drill? Do we meet in a bar that serves spirits and snacks?"

She bobbed her head again, slightly more patronisingly, I felt. It was a warning, I supposed, not to be too flippant.

"No, you'll have to come to Becca's. You see, he talks through her."

"Through her?"

"That's right! I cannot explain it very well but try looking up mediums on the internet in the library over there. If you could come this evening, it would be lovely of you. It's not far, only on Sunset."

In Los Angeles the phrase "on Sunset" meant something rather different to the well-kept 1920s semis that led from the top of the Denmark Hill to Ruskin Park, which were served by the P4 bus. Anywhere rejoicing in the name Sunset Road, when the name was not ironically applied to a valley-bottom slum or rain-drenched mountainside, should have been an upbeat spot but Sunset Road SE5 positively beamed and the streets around it were pretty as well.

I took her advice and did a spot of séance wikiing. The word derived from Old French seoir, meaning to sit. In English it was used in connection with receiving messages from the dead or, in the language used by practitioners, those who had passed over. The medium was the person who contacted the spirit world and acted as a conduit between it and ours. Not all spirits talked directly so I was prepared to encounter automatic writing, numbered raps, levitation or the improbable sounding spirit trumpets.

Armed with this information and a certain amount of native scepticism (reinforced by the research) I got off the P4 that evening and made my way to a stained glass door, having first paused to admire the well-kept garden. I had half expected an ivy darkened pile but the house was in no way distinguishable from the other residences. I was shown in by a short white lady in a turban and one of the beakiest noses I'd ever seen. She swished me through the hall and indicated a room to the right.

"Becca is in there. We've just started and Ben's terribly anxious to meet you."

I tried to ignore the casual way in which she conflated a living friend with a dead pugilist as I stepped into a warm, badly lit sitting room. There was a small table around which sat the acquaintance from the library, an earnest looking West Indian lady and, at the centre, a tall woman with a young face, grey hair and saucily painted lips. This, apparently, was Becca.

I took a chair opposite Becca, who nodded at me then abruptly rolled her eyes back as she entered into a trance. The others would record what was said as, I understood, Becca would have no recollection of it. That was handy for me as it meant I'd not have to bother with notes. Becca's head lolled and I was put in mind of the old rope-a-dope tactic of the great Muhammad Ali but suddenly she snapped to attention and started to speak.

It was not the voice I'd expected to hear. The accent was more rustic, sort of Kidderminster by way of Kent, and there was a softness to it, of tone at least. Underpinning the words, though, was a force and a stubborn will that, I reflected, one would need to have if one wanted to make the journey from the underworld.

"You the journalist cove?" It came out "Yo da jernaleest cove?"

One of the ladies indicated that I should reply so I started out with some respect but a quick jab.

"I am. And do I have the honour of addressing Ben Caunt, several times champion of England and alleged world heavyweight champ?"

When interviewing living boxers it was customary to start with their triumphs before probing the more controversial aspects of their career. The reason for this custom was that, while fighters may have retired from the ring, they remained prone to violence and time rarely diminished the ego. I decided to reverse this on the not unreasonable grounds that I was unlikely to receive a beating from a ghost.

"No alleged about it! Our talk will settle the matter once and for all," Caunt replied levelly.

He had taken my first query on the chin. I followed up with a question about his disputed disqualification in 1835 for belting William "Bendigo" Thompson while he was sitting in his corner.

Caunt replied that such activities were normal and it reflected badly on Thompson for making a big fuss. Further, he said that Thompson had something of the schoolgirl about him for going down in the seventy-fifth round three years later at Skipworth Common. This was the fight that, in Caunt's mind at least, won him the heavyweight championship of England, especially as Thompson had swerved the rematch.

Through Becca's mediumship, Caunt got quickly into his stride, recalling the one hundred and one rounds he went against Bill Brassey at the splendidly named Six Mile Bottom. He also, after prodding, acknowledged that he had fought a bit dirty against Nick Ward in 1841, when the crowd had howled for his disqualification. He admitted striking Ward while he was down but pointed out that he had won the rematch a few months later in thirty-five rounds, which made him English champion. In this role he travelled to the US and challenged the American Tom Hyer, who declined to fight. Caunt then claimed the world championship by default, but his claim was not widely upheld.

Unlike most boxers I'd interviewed – hunched over their whiskies, bitter and maudlin about the past – Caunt was upbeat. He even managed to skip over one major event in his life: his departure from it in 1861, as the result of pneumonia. Of course, I couldn't discount the effect Becca's jaunty character had (judging by her clothes and slap) in moderating his comments.

In 1845, after a tough battle against old foe William Thompson, Caunt quit fighting and worked for a time as a labourer before becoming landlord of the Coach and Horses in St Martin's Lane. He recalled this as the most contented and prosperous time of his life but it all fell apart when a fire destroyed his livelihood and killed two of his children. In 1857, at the age of forty-two, he rejoined the circuit of bare-knuckle scrapping with a sixty-round bout. As I listened to him talking about this fight I started to wonder about Caunt's recollection of events. As was the case for all former fighters I'd ever encountered, one had to make allowances for the possibility of mental impairment after a lifetime of receiving violent blows to the head.

In the middle of describing the bout, he paused. I assumed (I was getting used to the language by now) that the connection with the other side had been broken, but it was just a tangential change in subject. If he'd been sitting in front of me I'd have noticed the symptoms earlier – the wandering eyes, shaking hands and perplexed expression of the afflicted ex-pugilist. I just had the voice and story to go on, so I was slower to catch on but the signs were unmistakable. I realised the time-frame had changed and he was no longer talking about his heyday a century-and-a-half past, but a fight that seemed to have taken place that year. I thought of my gran in her eighties, in her mind still living in the Liverpool of her youth in the 1930s.

"Of course," I was still struggling with the fact that the voice of a Victorian bruiser was emanating from a grey lady in a lively shirt, "we had to change the judging a bit for the recent contests."

Prior to the pause, Caunt had been talking about how fights carried on until one or the other couldn't get up. It was not then the textbook martial art and combat sport in which two people engaged in a contest of strength, reflexes and endurance by throwing punches at an opponent with the goal of a knock-out with gloved hands. No gloves, for a start. It turned out that there had been none in his recent match either.

"This summer was more like shadow boxing, which I suppose it was, technically. It was all feints and glancing blows and no hitting through the belt. It was pretty daft; we could literally punch holes into each other!"

"Lie-ter-ally paunch 'oles into each ohther" was how it came out.

There then came what I assumed was a chuckle but, filtered through the guts of a Denmark Hill dame, it emerged more like a strangled wheeze.

He recovered to add that there had been lots of slipping (which in boxing meant rotating the body slightly so that an incoming punch passed harmlessly next to the head) and sway or fade (meaning anticipating a punch and moving the upper body or head back so that it missed).

I quizzed him more about this modern-day contest, possibly the first Ben Caunt fight since a sixty-rounder against Nat Langham had been declared a draw in the middle of the nineteenth century. What followed was really eye opening.

"We had fewer problems with judging and venues than some of the other events. There were arguments about how to measure and rank walking through walls, crockery throwing", he paused, "and chain rattling had problems with noise and assessing style."

There was another lull where I wondered where Ben had learned the concept of style assessment.

"For the boxing, we just drifted into the old Empire Stadium and carried on. But some of the events were in the open air and we didn't want people seeing. By people I mean your lot. The living, as it were."

I parried to give me time to think. "Chain rattling? Crockery throwing?"

"They were easy venue-wise because they were indoors. The water sports and other outdoor events proved more challenging as they needed to be accessible. They had to have a certain charm and atmosphere." He paused again. "I mean, you don't want prestigious visitors from all over the globe pitching up on some abandoned industrial estate in Ponders End do you?"

"Visitors?" I queried, "From overseas?"

"They were once from abroad but, in reality, they came through the vale like I did. They wanted to visit and as hosts of the event we started with several advantages and disadvantages. London is already one of the most haunted places on the planet and a popular destination for foreign spectres. In terms of legacy, we wanted a showcase for some innovative haunting as well as excelling in the traditional crafts."

There was a minor noise at the door, which distracted everyone.

"Cat trying to get in. Seems to like Ben for some reason," explained the beaky nosed lady.

Ben, who had paused, piped up again.

"We were also keen not to disrupt the everyday routine of our local spirits, who play their part in the economy."

At this juncture, one of the ladies pushed a piece of paper my way. On it was detailed the exact scale of the paranormal economy, from ghost walks, haunted venue tours, phantom hunts and attendant merchandising. It was an impressive total.

Ben picked up his theme. "On top of this, we were anxious to avoid panic amongst the city's other residents" (which I took to mean me). "You can appreciate that with thousands of shades on the loose, all keen to visit London's favourite landmarks, incidents might occur. I think we handled it rather well, all things considered. There were a few reports in the press but nothing major. That Jessica Ennis saved us – reporters had little time for anything else."

He drifted off again and was trying to grasp at something to get back to his original story but the journalist in me was already sniffing at a bigger one so I tried, in the language of the profession, to open a cut that wouldn't close.

"So you are telling me that there was a convention of what? Apparitions? Wraiths? Phantoms? Frights? Horrors?" I struggled to think of more before weakly adding, "Banshees?"

He absorbed the onslaught and pointed out that some of those words carried negative associations. The preferred term, apparently, is revenant British or revenant citizen but he did concede that there were banshees present and, unsurprisingly, the Irish ones had won the gold in the screaming diabolically at night event.

Despite my head feeling that it had gone several physical rounds with Ben in his pomp, I was just about to retaliate when the lady from the library intervened. She pushed a couple of typed pages across to me and said, "We pieced together most of the events and venues and collated them here."

I looked at her, then at the smiling Becca and finally at the sheets of paper. One was a list of activities, together with gold, silver and bronze winners, and the other listed the venues that had been chosen. These ranged from the predictable to the improbable but I considered that ghosts might have a different sense of what constituted a good venue. Amongst those cited were the Heygate Estate, Barnes Common, Beverley Brook, Windsor Castle, West Norwood Cemetery, Tower of London, River Walbrook, Adelphi Theatre, York Road Station, British Museum and Highgate Woods.

Ben anticipated my question.

"It was all thought through in terms of logistics and spectators," he said. "We even ran a ghost train up the old line from Finsbury Park to Highgate."

I turned my attention to the contests (I couldn't bring myself to use the word sport). These included: the *deadcathlon*, *chain rattling* (as mentioned), something called *heavy clumping*, *knocking on wood*, the *water glide* (won by the Hungarians for a synchronised haint across Shadwell Basin), *hovering* (vertical and horizontal), *passing through walls*, *throwing crockery* (in which a team of German poltergeists triumphed), the *hauntathlon* and *wailing*. I couldn't read much more and wasn't sure I knew, or even wanted to know, what *original manifestation* could entail.

The West Indian lady chipped in. "There were regular events too. Ghost hockey, football and, obviously, boxing. That's what Ben wanted you for. You see, for him, the rest of the Paranormal Games was a bit of a side show."

"Side show?" I muttered.

"Yes!" Ben was talking again. "For me it was all about settling an age-old score. I need you to sort that in the record books. The *proper boxing record books*." He emphasised the last part.

"You see, I won the gold against that wretch Bill "Bendigo" Thompson, which makes me not only a top medallist but also undisputed heavyweight champion of the world!"

It was the knockout blow for me. Big Ben had come from behind again and won, whilst all summer we had been ghosting the games.

I Thought We Was Fam

Part One: The ends

My name is Jonah and I'm not sure anyone else believes my little sister Joana is not a murderer, but I do. The two of us take the 185 bus to the courthouse to give us one last chance to reflect on events. I want to linger on our memories, think them over, reflect on them and, possibly in time, relive them because, sometimes, shared memories are what make us. Those, and where you come from.

The 185 to Camberwell travels through all the roaring twenties, from Honor Oak to the Champion Hill Estate via Dog Kennel Hill, and Dawson Heights. Football fans from Dulwich Hamlet call our area Tuscany but we call it the roaring twenties of Mumbai, referring to the estates in SE22, SE23 and SE24. I've no idea why South London estates rebrand themselves as faraway places, Harlem (Kennington Park) or Moscow (the Brandon in Walworth), but they do.

Like the film *Warriors*, each estate has its own crew and the sparkly graffiti to prove it, as well as broken metal steeds of orange and yellow or, more rarely, red. Each estate has its puddles of votive flowers or commemorative Stone Island tops, messages to the fallen scrawled in defiance, anger and love. Before local councils banned such practices, there used to be murals with words of tribute to those who had been killed but there have become so many of them it seems that wall space has got to be in short supply. The flowers wither, the clothing corrodes and the messages fade, except in the hearts of the loved and the vengeful.

Joana will not be taking the option of that other bus, the one they offer to Azkaban so, as a result, she'll get a proper stretch. If she's lucky she could be out by the time she's thirty; if not, she'll be more like forty. We've discussed it though and we've decided that Azkaban is worse. It means a year and a half to life, you might say. Joana's lawyer has suggested she goes for the mental health defence but, thing is, she's not mental.

In case you're wondering, Azkaban ain't a place. Well, it is, but that's not its real name. It's just what we call it since we saw the *Harry Potter* films. One day it wasn't there; the next it was. It's an experimental rehabilitation facility on a remote Scottish island, no visitors, no communication out. Drones are shot down before they get close and there are rumours of a failed attempt by a crew from Liverpool to access it by boat. It is a magic place where strange things happen. People come back after eighteen months totally different, all calm and transformed. The worst of the worst of the worst bad boys and girls, all turned around and citizen-like.

Azkaban offers hard work, isolation, therapy and positive results. All you do is agree to the terms and your sentence is reduced to a year and a half. Most regular people love it as a solution to the knife murder problem and even those who at first fumed over the short sentences were won over when the offending levels fell off, the murder rate spiked and declined, and the knife times ended.

Except for Joana. And who is she anyway? This is her story, and mine, but what she keeps stressing on the 185 is that she is a good girl. That she still is a good girl.

I agree. She is, and not just because she's my sister.

It was when Joana and I were at secondary school that our area changed almost overnight – at least, that's how it felt. Mum used to say it turned from Safeway to Sainsbury's. I can't remember what Safeway even was but I know what she meant. Restaurants opened, pubs cleaned their windows and, strangest of all, there were posh pregnant white women everywhere. New shops opened selling what our Granny Black called "fancy goods" and Granny White, through her gummy mouth, called "gee gaws".

On the estates, for the most part, the old cycle of life continued but mum encouraged Joana to get a holiday job in a shop that sold expensive plates, lampshades and curtains. The owner of the shop had a friend who needed staff for a wine store, East Dulwich Liquor, and so on her sixteenth birthday Joana started there three evenings a week.

Joana was better at school than I was, but she said the wine shop was a real education, and not just in terms of wine or retail, or "customer relations and sales" as she used to call it. She could talk her way around a vineyard with the best of them, but her real schooling was in people. In particular she got to see how rich (mostly) white people were and how they saw her. Joana was a sort of protégé, cypher, fig leaf and muse. She used to have us in pieces when she described how awkward or patronising some of the customers were. She was their token, their sounding board and, sometimes, their confidante. She'd got the voices just right.

"My daughter's doing... Most marvellous girl off the estate... What does 'ends' mean?... Is road knowledge the same as street knowledge?"

If it had been me and I was that clever, I might have taken liberties, but she didn't, she just saw an opportunity to keep on learning.

It was through the shop that she met Dis "Dee" Coba.

Dee was in my year at school but we were never fam. Joana was taken with Dee's clever eyes and a smile she described as "going four ways at once". She claimed that life, humour and joy just bounced from him. I had my own opinions of Dee, not all bad, but I was not excited at being his brother in law.

Dee and his crew, Mumbai20s, had gone to East Dulwich Liquor to buy some celebratory drinks but when one of them started boosting Cristal Champagne, Joana intervened. She told her friends about it later and quoted herself with delight amidst encouraging laughter from her mates. I remember sitting there while she ran through the story for, at least, the third time.

"So I said, 'You could go for Cristal but I think for value and taste you'd be better with the sekt Piper-Heidsieck, which is dryer'. I stopped there and made sure I had their attention, then I said, 'If you want something extra special go for the Veuve Clicquot. People pick Cristal because they don't know any better, but you guys look like in most things you do.' And they were like all silent, innit? So I said, 'Or, at least you deserve better'. Swear down that was the killer. They all laughed. There was talk of shortie sorts speaking up but I'd won them over innit?

"Upsold and more sold. They bought four bottles, then Dee said, 'Hey I know you, you're Jonah's sister. When did you get to be all so clever and fit?'

"I just smiled, innit. I ruled it!"

I heard a similar version from the guy who owned the shop, Edward ("Call me Ted"), who had observed the whole exchange.

Ted, who is camper than the outdoor living section at Decathlon, had clapped his hands and laughed at it all, like he'd stumbled on a mating ritual of an exotic tribe rather than some people from just up the road.

Joana related Ted's reaction as well.

"My girl," she quoted getting his slight Scottish accent to perfection, "that was simply marvellous. You are simply marvellous."

She was properly full of herself then. I wanted to be happy for her but, she is my sister and Dee had a reputation.

****

Part Two: The rise

Joana loved being a part of the video shoots on local estates for Dee's tunes and I must admit that boy could spit bars and had an eye for drama. His relationship with Joana grew alongside the excitement of rising downloads, streams and hits for Mumbai20s.

Joana's role at the wine shop changed as well, so she was more involved in supplying drinks for events, dealing with pubs and restaurants and the online marketing that went with it. She transferred some of the skills she learned at the shop to the marketing of Mumbai20s. The fierce evening with our mum when Joana announced that she was deferring university came as no surprise to me. Her argument in favour of a delay was that the life she led was a schooling that paid. Joana even made a minor contribution to the music, a steal and sample from Dorothy Parker's *Resumé*:

> *Knives they a pain you and drugs we a ramp.*
> *Acids a stain you, doan carry a shank.*
> *Gats are well naff and nooses a give.*
> *Gas make you giraffe, you might as well live.*

Joana loved flexing with all sorts and the crew's name attracted jazz heads from the real Mumbai, who enquired online about links to the underground Raj jazz scene. World music types asked about tours and festival appearances, and there were even people who detected a 'twenties vibe to the music. In response to that, the crew released Ghetto Charleston, complete with dance steps, which featured Joana and a few of our cousins.

Sometimes Joana or Dee would make up a fake musical history and roots but mainly they just described what they did as "a London something". Because whatever the move from jungle to speed garage to dubstep to 2-step to grime and on to drill, it was all about South London and the roaring twenties. The place you smoke your first gear, kiss your first love and know the ways, manners, codes and people – we call that road knowledge. A part of me loved it that Dee (and Joana and the rest) repped us so well and were known across the southern ends and even on the east side.

Dee had come up harder than the pair of us and had greater road knowledge but Joana and he shared good business brains, a love of words and what in a traditional career path might be described as excellent marketing skills. Words were the thing that bound them, not just the glorying in southside patois but the richness of Shakespearian English and the power of vocabulary.

Dee told Joana about something called a shibboleth and how it was used as a sort of pass code by the Hebrews. If you understood it, and pronounced it correctly, you were fam. I remember it as a computer log-in system at school, but it could be any custom or tradition that distinguishes one group of people (an ingroup) from others (outgroups). Joana played me a scene from *The Wire* TV show in which a Baltimore firm of drug dealers used their knowledge of local radio stations to distinguish themselves from encroaching New Yorkers.

Dee wrote a song about the shibboleth, called *Mumbai Messy*. It was a celebration of our area and its cultural distinctions, as well as what might happen to those who are *in* ends but not *of* ends. We all loved it, it was an anthem for us, like a theme tune. There was a line in *Mumbai Messy* that was to haunt us, though we didn't know it at the time.

The most famous resident of our manor is an overstuffed walrus at the local museum. We'd all been on countless school trips and knew that the reason it was so huge was that the people doing the taxidermy had never seen a real walrus. This meant they stuffed it to capacity rather than allowing its skin to be loose, as it is in nature. Knowing this was, if you like, a shibboleth, and one that Dee celebrated with the line:

> *Chief who don't know why the walrus fat,*
> *Chief could get wet for not knowing that.*

****

Part Three: The fall

The bad thing happened in the Greendale. The Greendale is a bit of woodland and meadow crossed by paths and cycle routes at the back of Dulwich Hamlet's ground. I once heard it described as a transitional zone which, when I looked the meaning up seemed about right. A no man's land, where people moved freely between postcodes until a firm up from Seven Bridge Town, Loughborough Junction, decided to change that.

Five young lads belonging to the SBT Young Boys jumped Dee and his cousin Agwe with blades. Agwe was killed and Dee escaped up Abbotswood to Edgar Krail Way and into Sainsburys, but only after he wet one of theirs by slashing him across the throat with a knife of his own.

The police soon came for Dee for, whilst the Dale may be CCTV free, the surrounding areas are not. The police search not only turned up the weapon Dee used but also an arsenal of hidden knives and drugs. Joana raged and cursed – Dee had sworn that he didn't carry anymore and one time, after he made bail, I had to step up between them as she furiously attacked him.

Joana alternated between grief and fury. Sometimes she tried to front up with a cold detachment at the horrible inevitability of it all. Dee's talent and popularity were a source of envy and resentment, not just for rival firms in Peckham, Brixton and Camberwell but also those in our own ends who saw his downfall as an opportunity. Dee once predicted as much in a bar that ran:

> *When man a great sheik all want his aid,*
> *When the great sheik dead them a cast much shade.*

That line was quoted in the trial by the defence, to suggest Dee's need to protect himself. The prosecution ran stronger with the walrus line, arguing that in the lyric Dee was clearly threatening those from outside the area. The lawyer for the prosecution explained to the judge the meaning:

"To wet, my lord, means to stab, to cause blood to flow and make the person wet. Some of their kind joke about going out with waterproofs on for such knifing missions to prevent their own precious clothing from getting blood on them."

The prosecution prevailed and Dee took the Azkaban route of eighteen months in preference to an eighteen-year prison sentence. The road wisdom, and that of most legal advisors, was that it was the best option and, despite the dark jokes and stories that had been seeping out about it, everybody knew there were no such thing as dementors.

Joana focused on her work at Ted's, who was genuinely concerned: "That poor girl... Tried her best by everyone... My heart goes out..." Knowing Joana's sense of independence, he and I tried discreetly to help her.

One thing Ted and Joana did together was their campaign against knife crime. Joana was in the papers a lot and used her different networks to set up projects connecting the posh types to the estates via Ted and the shop. I'm not sure I liked one of her jingles ("*Not a knife, just a fork and a bottle and a cork*") but I'm told it appealed to the dinner party circuits of the Rye, Herne Hill and Lordship Lane.

Mum and I were really proud when Joana won an award from the Evening Standard. I thought she was getting over Dee and moving on, and we all hoped for better times ahead.

Then Dee came back. His last words to both of us had been that stupid quote from *The Wire*: "You only do two days. The day you go in and the day you leave."

For Joana it had been much longer than two days, and there had been much water under many bridges and many tears in addition. However, even after eighteen months she was keen to make the relationship work. Dee was her love and needed her support. I know she cast some harsh words in his direction but she had prepared herself as best could by networking with other Azkaban "widows" and recently reunited couples and families.

They helped her through possibly the hardest bit of Azkaban, which was the absence of any outward communication; only letters in were allowed. It was part of the deal that Dee, and everyone else who went there, signed up to.

I'm certain Joana's thorough preparation helped and, to my surprise, at first everything seemed to go well and fit the storyline she had built – of a reformed gang member joining his partner in an anti-knife-crime crusade. Dee didn't speak much about Azkaban to either of us or any of the crew, but Joana liked what he did say about sheep that ate seaweed, learning country skills and things from boat parts to pineapples that washed up on the beach. I was less charmed at her confession that Dee had come back fitter and filed this under "too much information".

They got a housing association flat together on the Dog Kennel Hill Estate. I went to the flat warming, an uneasy mix of street and posh with Ted presiding. Several key campaign supporters were present but the rest of us relaxed when they left and we could openly check out the various well-wisher gifts they'd brought to help set up the flat. Joana was right on it with the accent impersonations when I asked her about them.

" 'Well darling, we really don't need two sets, our eldest got married last year and we've just got too much stuff...' 'Oh, my brother's in the business and these are just client gift leftovers...'"

I got the impression that some of the furniture, cutlery and crockery was a bit too well matched and thought out. It was more like a wedding list but in truth I know nothing of the affluent and their charity, and I noticed the other partners of Azkaban "graduates" were impressed. I also noted how little time the former detainees had for each other. I've been at parties where there were former jailbirds before – not often, but statistically growing up in ends it's bound to happen – and however suspicious they are of each other they always bond over time spent inside. The Azkaban lot never spoke together. I assumed this was part of the treatment.

When things went wrong between Joana and Dee, the people she turned to, apart from myself and the rest of the family, were the other Azkaban partners. I took the bus with her that time as well, the 185 through Mumbai and Moscow to Harlem where we met up with Paulette Vancy, whose partner had been back for a year longer than Dee. Paulette was skinny, tall, brittlely pretty and, I guessed, a decade older than Joana.

We met in the café in Kennington Park, which alongside the rest of us, like much of that part of South London, was full of Latinos and Portuguese. We were joined by Abigay who lived on the Brandon Estate just east of the park and whose grandson had spent time on the island. Abigay had encouraged her grandson to go to church with her at the beautiful Calvary Temple on Councillor Street. He'd been a very religious young boy till his teenage years, and she considered it strange that, in his transformation from teenage terror to mature young man, he'd forgotten his scriptures.

Paulette nodded and said that there were some words she'd had to explain to her man.

"You know what it's like with chat. Meanings change quick and everybody picks up the new ones. Well it's like he's lost the ability to do that. Christ, it's like someone saying "safe" or summat else from another era. I keep having to translate."

She stubbed her cigarette out and looked at all of us.

"Why don't we stop dancing around this? Our men, our boys, are not what they were and I'm sort of okay with that. He doesn't cheat me, he doesn't beat me, he spends time with his boys and he brings home honest dollar. Oh," she added as an afterthought that made me blush, "and the sex is better, he's more patient and never too fucked up."

Joana sat very still. Abigay said, "You mean, what? They're not real? They're not human? How is that?"

"Look, you said he was different. Maybe there is a bit in there of him, like, what say aye eye. Artificial..." Paulette hesitated.

"Artificial intelligence," Joana completed the sentence.

"I can see you judging me but I've thought this through. It makes sense," Paulette continued.

"I'm not judging you," Joana said. As for me, I thought that it all fitted, even though Dee looked so real and, I guessed for Joana, felt real.

"I know what you're thinking – but if you cut me do I bleed? Does he?"

We left the others and walked in silence past the tennis courts. Saying the words was one thing but the rest was too big.

Joana sighed and said, "It's the chat, it's about the vocabulary! Dee's lost all his poetry, all his word vision."

The worst thing happened a fortnight later and, in the end, it was the shibboleth that gave it away, not Dee's inability to learn the latest words. When Joana asked him about the word shibboleth itself, he had no idea what she meant.

Joana reacted first.

They were in the kitchen and she picked up the knife they used to cut meat with. She wasn't sure whether he had slipped or lunged, or if she herself had slipped, but the knife went hilt-deep into his flesh by his pelvic bone. Joana phoned me and was still sobbing by the door when I arrived ten minutes later. She let me in and what I saw was much stranger than murder. There was no blood. Dee was moving jerkily in small circles around the kitchen. It was as if a circuit was broken and all he could do was make that manoeuvre and repeat,

"I thought we was fam. I thought we was fam. I thought we was fam."

****

Part Four: The end of ends

The 185 passes Denmark Hill Station and turns right downhill to Camberwell, the end of the roaring twenties. I look at Joana and say,

"I believe you but there is no way that they'll let out the secrets of Azkaban. Take the long stretch. That way, at least, at the end of all this *we* will still be fam."

The Liberty Bus

"Does it not strike *you* as odd, the positions of the cats? And yes, I will have a whisky please."

She smiled.

"I know what you are thinking. You are thinking that it's a bloody liberty my asking for a double whisky."

I blushed, laughed and altered the order upwards.

She wore a leather skirt that stopped just above knee high black boots, and a red silk shirt under a black velvet coat. She had dark wavy hair pulled back off her face and an eyepatch that refracted light from the rhinestones embedded in it.

Her voice was "dark brown", as in the song Lola by the Kinks. Once, when people smoked in bars, one might have imagined it accompanied by a blueish cloud, silky, smooth and sensual. I'd watched her with bemused detachment a few minutes earlier when she'd asked a question that stilled the room.

"What, in your opinion, is, if any, the significance of the cat statues, or symbols, at so many entrances to the city?"

It was delivered as if she knew the answer and was testing the lecturer, who, despite being an expert in animal folklore, clearly didn't. The compere also looked puzzled.

Into the silence she poured, "You spoke of Hodge, the Coade Stone Lion, Chaucer at Custom House and the sacrificed beast at Saint Michael Paternoster."

She paused, adjusted her position and added, "Not to mention the poor kitties that used to be at the Tower. I just wondered if you had a theory?"

The compere, a wily, thirsty man, was alive to the dangers of an open-ended speculative question and the delay it may cause him getting a drink. He suggested carrying on the discussion on the group's Facebook page, or at the bar. Several of the grey whiskered habitués were very keen to do that with her but that's when the questioner had approached me.

"'Liberties innit' is one of my favourite London phrases," she was saying. "It means someone, somewhere has in some way pushed boundaries, behaved incorrectly or caused offence. No one else uses the term in quite the same impassioned way as the aggrieved Cockney, and for no one else does it carry such weight of meaning, or indeed history."

She sidled closer. We clinked glasses.

I hadn't offered her a drink any more than it had occurred to me to consider the cats, but we chatted about the talk and the venue. The Queen Mary, moored at the Savoy Pier on the Thames, was a distinct improvement on the usual upstairs rooms in Borough pubs as a meeting place for LUOF (London Union of Folklore). It was only a six-month residency but the views of the river, South Bank and bridges were superb.

She told me she was born within the sound of Bow Bells. I said I worked near them, on the Walbrook by Cannon Street.

She replied, "Everyone has to start somewhere. My name is Claire. What's yours?"

I told her, "Bill, my name is Bill."

The topic of the night's talk had been London's beasts, both iconic and fabulous, from Chunee the Elephant executed after running amok on the Strand to the ravens at the Tower and the herds of feral albino swine in the covered rivers. There was mention of the legendary shape-shifting sorceress of the sewers, Queen Rat, who pops up in waterman folklore to spend an evening with mortals she fancies and reward the discreet ones. The felines mentioned in Claire's question had come up along with Faith, the church cat of St Augustine's, plus the black dog of Newgate and all manner of ghostly creatures from London's past and present.

We soon moved on and I was swept up with talking to Claire about dreams, futures and pasts. Mostly I spoke and when I asked her questions about her own past she just laughed, an inclusive engaging laugh that made light of everything, and joked, "I've more of it than you. I thought you'd be quicker. Plenty of time for that don't you think? Another drink?"

She was a bit older than myself but, I thought, no more than a decade, putting her in her mid to late thirties. I felt at ease with her but also odd, because it was unusual for me to attract women like this. I cynically considered that she might just have been looking to avoid the attentions of some of the old goats who attended the folklore meetings and could bore to Olympic standard given a chance.

I told her I lived on Fair Street, off Tooley, in a flat three doors down from the former home of serial killer Colin Ireland.

She smiled at this. "Death and Death and Death. Trapped between the Potters Fields and St Olave's cemetery. Poor you! You deserve some life."

She sipped her drink. "I live on Jacob's Island, so we should share a carriage home. The Rodent Vehicle One will do for both of us!"

The joke belied the instruction, but I would have agreed anyway. We rocked along the Embankment up to Waterloo Bridge and kissed with the river in the background.

The RV1 lurched up. She broke off the kiss with a gentle bite and we got on the bus.

"Ladies' prerogative on the ladies' bridge. Besides it's a sexy route the RV1. It links the Maiden Lanes of Covent Garden and the Borough, and continues on to the Tower Liberty. Four hundred years of legal brothels on Bankside then the Georgian and Victorian fleshpots of Lambeth's Lower Marsh and the twentieth-century station trade. Those would-be courtesans flocked over this bridge to The Strand."

She paused and stroked my thigh.

"Shocking. All that naughtiness."

I could almost sense the panting streets around me. Histories jostling for prominence, the Upper Ground, the Sandy Ford, the Hatter's Field, even Bear Alley and, tucked away, the most western of the old legal red light areas and home to the poshest bordellos, the Paris Gardens. All that flesh, I thought, and seekers of pleasure who disembarked at Barge House Stair and made their way through the marshes of the old South Work to the baited bears, the poor players and the dolly mopps.

Claire crossed her left leg to reveal some of her hosiery. Her talk was racy, jumbled and scary. I'm in for a treat I thought. I like this. She is my sort.

We got off at my flat and went upstairs. She approved of the view even though it was crimped by the new Greater London Authority building.

Claire took her eye patch off as the start of a longer striptease and winked. It was a beauty; slow, saucy, flirty and bright. I noticed that her eyes were different colours. One sparkled and rippled like a river in the sunlight, not the muddy Thames, but an azure stream of absolute clarity. The other was grey and misty, the river light that the painter Monet tried to capture.

I scrambled to take my clothes and turn the lights, off. She tore my cheek with her teeth and I felt shock, but not pain, as she bit my shoulder. I felt scratched all over as if she had two pairs of hands. I remember an ecstatically exciting time that carried on until near dawn.

I slept eventually and dreamt of the bus journey across Southwark through different eyes. Sometimes just vivid images, other times accompanied by Claire's voice in my ears.

"I wear an eye patch to stop the brain fever. I have two eyes just like you, but my eyes see things differently. My blue eye observes what you do; that is, people leaving work, heading to bars, theatres and home. With my grey eye, the purblind inner eye of the rat, I see the city as my rodent cousins do."

In my dreams I saw an enchanted London that was eternal, magic and quantum. Men hunted with horses whilst red kites circled the RV1 and badgers were led off to fight, there were falconers and performers from the first ever modern circus. I saw it all at once.

And it hurt. But it was beautiful.

I saw ravers pouring out of London's first acid house club in the 1980s. Ecstasy lent them euphoria and vision and amongst them a raven-haired beauty in an eye patch and smiley t-shirt. At the old Hop Exchange, hordes of office employees stood outside the pubs, and tours of strollers were guided past by mountebank street-chatterers bellowing a history they couldn't feel. There were Victorian gents in puffed up suits and whiskers and, nearby, orphaned waifs snatched at silks. I spotted the young Mr Dickens on his way to see the old Mr Dickens at the Marshalsea prison.

My nose twitched at the stench of the old London larder. Hops brewed, vinegar boiled, jam stewed and, pervading it all, the vile tang of flesh parted from skin with the aid of dog waste.

Half consciously I was wondering if smell was possible in a dream when her voice whispered, "You don't recognise me in any real sense as you are too bound up, constrained and focused on your day to day and the monies to be plucked from my streets. There have been artists, absinthe swallowers and the insane who have seen me, as well as the hatters, half mental with the mercury vapours they worked with. The toshers and mudlarks knew of me, though they barely dared whisper my name, a name that brought good fortune to some but nothing to many. I am the Queen, the Queen of Rats, and this is part of my manor. *My* liberties.

"I used to cross the river to that menagerie of beasts at the Tower and sidle up to the leopards and lions who lived there. Then, with a gesture to over the water, I would whisper into their stupid feline faces. It's my city, Kitty. Over there. It's my city."

When I fully woke it was to an intense nip behind my ear and the sight of her leaving the flat, but her voice remained in my head, like a delayed send off or memory.

"Love, from its very nature, must be transitory. To seek for a secret that would render it constant would be as wild a search as for the philosopher's stone or the grand panacea: and the discovery would be equally useless or, rather, pernicious. You'll not speak of this sharp sweetness but let it stew and savour in your heart and something tangible will emerge."

The answer to the question about cats that she had posed at the meeting popped into my head. I thought it better not to tell anyone. I would say I'd cut myself shaving if anyone asked about the marks on my face and neck.

Postscript, 2019

I live in Bristol now with my wife, Trudy, and three children, Tilly and the twins. We decided to take a long weekend trip to coincide with a morning meeting I had at my old office near the Thames. Trudy dropped the children off with me at lunchtime and, while she went shopping, I took them skating at the Tower. The plan was for us all to meet up again for a meal and a show in the evening.

It was a bright, clear December day as the four of us walked to Southwark Bridge and along past the last working dock in central London, where the rubbish from the City is loaded onto barges and shipped out.

My eldest, Tilly, sniffed the air, ran along the foreshore and drank it all in. It was her first trip to London's Thames, and she scampered below the embankments and explored as far as she could, right up to the water's edge. She was excited by the boats and, more disturbingly, by the piles of bones collected underneath Cannon Street Railway Bridge. It was as if every restaurant in London had dumped its leftovers into the sewers for centuries and they'd all flushed out there, near the outfall of the River Walbrook. Chicken bones, bits of cattle skeleton, sheep bones, even what looked like fossilised horse and oxen parts.

Tilly is an adventurous child, keen to explore new things and places and different from the twins, who are a couple of years her junior. They have far more of my wife in their make-up, almost to the point where Trudy jokes that Tilly was brought by the fairies.

The twins spotted the rat first and drew back. Tilly, however, stood quite still and stared at it, curious and confident. The rodent, which was the size of a fully-grown tomcat, raised its paw first towards Tilly then to myself, before it disappeared behind one of the moored boats that rested on the exposed riverbed. I'd seen a big rat before, long before Tilly and the twins arrived on the scene, when I went out by the Walbrook Stair to smoke or eat lunch. It surely couldn't be the same one after all these years.

As I looked at the rat I had another memory, of a woman in a velvet coat and eyepatch covering a grey eye that she'd insisted could see other worlds. Of being kissed gently on my torn flesh and her saying, "I expect we'll see each other again one of these days".

I remembered an eye that sparkled and rippled like a river in the sunlight. Not the muddy Thames, but an azure stream of absolute clarity. Very like Tilly's, in fact.

Jeux Sans Frontier

From the number 63 bus, as it swerves high over the old canal just before leaving Burgess Park, you can see the site of the Toymaker's House. It recently featured on a television design show for its use of space and, it must be said, it is unrecognisable now from the 1960s family home I remember when I was growing up. The adapted building now has a glass frontage and balconies, as well as a sunken garden, illuminated by the cunning use of light shafts.

My gran remembers further back in time, to the original Victorian canalside house in which the Toymaker once lived. She played in it after the war. She is too young to have visited the legendary shop on Rye Lane, full of wonderful clockwork trams that swayed like the real thing and were decorated to reflect the local routes. Nor did she see the displays of beautiful dolls in gorgeous dresses that people travelled from as far as Battersea to buy. She recalls the older children speaking of how, at the back of the store, there were marvellous puppets and dazzling glinting marbles, ruby reds, sapphire blues and diamond yellows.

The Toymaker made some of these marvels and some were manufactured locally, but he bought the rest from the great toy market at Lille, which he visited every year, disappearing for a month just after the start of school in September. He would return in October, in time for the half-term holiday, to prepare for the arrival of the new stock from abroad.

One year, before the German teddies, stuffed monkeys, Austrian and Russian curios, Turkish instruments and more of those superb marbles arrived at the shop, the Toymaker returned with a doll of his own. She was short, trim, well painted and beautifully clothed, as well as very, very French, though she spoke excellent English. The Toymaker introduced her as his wife, Estelle.

The Peckhamites didn't know what to make of this chic woman, who was not too young but a bit younger than the Toymaker. Estelle soon acquired a small dog, which the local children loved, and with which she would strut around the neighbourhood, looking vaguely as if there was a bad smell underneath her nose. Given the proximity of the canal that might have been understandable to the locals but over time a combination of jealousy, xenophobia and boredom turned many of them against her. On top of that they weren't too happy about the Toymaker changing the name of the shop from The Peckham Toy Shop to Jeux Sans Frontiers.

The Toymaker walked to work every day, a short commute along the tow path to where the library is now, picking up any provisions he needed at the Rye shops. At least, that was arrangement until the outbreak of the Second World War when he signed up to the army and ended up in Africa.

London was awash with foreign soldiers, including many of the Free French, and this proved a temptation for Estelle. Perhaps the fear of bombs hitting the canalside docks of Peckham and Walworth engendered reckless behaviour in her, or maybe this was her true nature, which had been smothered under the Toymaker's gentle respectability. Either way, she became a regular on the late trams to Haymarket and the Strand and local gossips noted that she certainly seemed to be doing her bit for the Entente Cordial, not to mention any number of special relationships with Americans.

High-explosive bombs landed on Bianca Road, Trafalgar Street and St George's Way in the winter of 1940, almost triangulating the Toymaker's house. Respite from the bombardment came in the summer of 1941 when the Toymaker had his first stretch of leave. Thus, through their shattered walls and badly fixed windows, the neighbours could take a break from the home service on the wireless and tune in to the Toymaker and Estelle story.

His first night home was merely tense, with a few slammed doors. The next day the Toymaker walked to his shop, which had struggled along with aging staff and a scarcity of new stock. That evening, after a few drinks at the Kentish Drovers, he returned to his house with a bag of toys he planned to take with him as gifts for his army pals' children.

The shouting started shortly after and continued throughout the remainder of his short stay.

His return on leave in 1942 was a little better except that by then Estelle had a friend staying – another French woman – and this time neighbours reported the two women shouting. Some described what they thought were the sounds of a beating and the Toymaker begging for mercy. The women, it seemed, were taunting him, but as none of the adults spoke French it wasn't clear what was being said. My gran's cousin, who was learning the language, claimed she could pick out a few phrases:

"Sur les genoux ver!" *"Bow à vos maîtresses."* *"Lécher ses bottes."*
No one believed her when she translated them:

"On your knees, worm!" "Bow to your mistresses." And "Lick her boots!"

Some felt that my gran's cousin was wasting time at school if that was the best she could come up with.

When the Toymaker limped home in late 1944, Estelle's friend had gone. He wasn't to see the final assault on Berlin but he did witness Hitler's final assault on London as Surrey rocked to doodle bugs and V-weapons. Among the victims of this onslaught was the small shop in a London suburb, once famed for its German teddy bears, Austrian clocks and pan-European jigsaws the like of which, ironically, a young Adolf Hitler might have played with as a child.

Two nights after Jeux Sans Frontiers was gutted, a stray piece of an intercepted missile damaged the Toymaker's home.

Early the next morning, a woman holding her small child, who was suffering from colic and couldn't sleep, witnessed two figures near the canal. They embraced briefly and headed in opposite directions: the Toymaker went south towards the Rye, Estelle north to the city. The child was my gran, who swears she remembers this.

The Toymaker's house, like so many others, was hastily boarded up and left to await the decision to demolish or repair. Teenagers broke in first and used it as a dry place to smoke and fumble. After these pioneers came younger children looking for somewhere sheltered to play in or hide from chore-demanding mothers. Thus it was the venue for games of hide and seek, cards and marbles by day, and more grown up activities in the evening.

One day a game of marbles took place in the main bedroom on a higher floor than my gran would normally climb. This room overlooked the canal and featured a fireplace with a dainty surround. At my gran's turn she scattered the balls away from the circle. Most rolled off towards the window, but some went over to the fireplace and there, as she bent to collect her winnings, she picked up a beautiful red marble she didn't remember seeing before. The next game the same thing happened; my gran won and this time found two extra marbles. Others won mystery marbles, too, which appeared to be coming out of the chimney.

The children of Peckham had been raised on talk of "the Toymaker's treasure" and the beautiful shop that once adorned Rye Lane. My gran and her friends resolved to tell no one else and return the following day to search the floorboards and walls for the lost toys.

But there was no next day. When the children gathered there after school, they found the house securely boarded and all the entrances blocked. My gran swears it was Neil Phillips, one of the others to win the strange marbles, who blabbed.

Gran wasn't clear about what prompted the adults to act but a week later some men from the council appeared and prioritised the house's demolition. A month after that, a team was sent in to take the building apart, starting with the upstairs rooms. Work was halted when, part of the way up the main chimney, they found the remains of a baby, its mouth stuffed with beautiful red marbles.

Slouching to Balham High Road

Durexic Park, so called on account of the number of used condoms on display, is on the other side of the tracks from Tooting Lido, that facsimile seaside of grassy reaches and clean-limbed desire. When I was young my friends and I dared each other to go there, past the courting couples, bodies for sale or rent and the sort of strange men your mother warned you about.

It continues to fascinate me now as it did then and, as a documentary film maker, I returned to make a short feature about the dark side of the Norbury and South Croydon line or, if you prefer, the 315 bus route. I like my career. It enables me to travel and live well, and it allowed me to return to the place that first steered me towards investigative journalism. Most of my oeuvre will never get the merest sniff of a BAFTA and the series of which this programme is a part, **UK's Most Haunted Woodlands**™, is unlikely to do so either.

Opposite the Common on Bedford Hill is the Priory. Today it heaves with the comfortable middle aged and their offspring, yet once it was the site of murder, debauchery and alleged witchcraft. In 1876, barrister Charles Delauney Turner Bravo was poisoned there, and lurid reports emerged of drunkenness, depravity and unspecified degrading sexual acts. No one was convicted for Bravo's death but amongst the suspects were his louche wife Florence, who, according to certain sources, was a bona fide witch with one dead husband already behind her. Also in the frame were her lover, society physician and abortionist, James Manby Gully, and her companion, Mrs Jane Cannon Cox, who the police branded a liar during their investigation.

Gully and Cox both fled the country and Florence drank herself to death within a couple of years of Charles Bravo being interred in West Norwood Cemetery. And while Florence's own final resting place remained a mystery, it was not her unquiet spirit that disturbed the peace of the Common but rather a fiend she brought into the world and some believed still walked upon it.

The first accounts of a creature on the Common appeared in the Victorian Penny Dreadful publications, then re-emerged in the local papers in the 1940s, buried amongst the war news. Reports in the rest of the twentieth century were limited to a passing reference in a punk fanzine reviewing a band called Monster on the Common (Oh Yeah) from the late 1970s.

Now, however, there was fresh news that an uncanny being had been spotted strolling about SW17 – and it wasn't a mummy, despite Tooting Common being every Egyptian's favourite London park. The rumours first popped up on Fortean message boards and social media, and these were followed up by features in several small publications and blog sites devoted to the supernatural. The sources of the stories were primarily the Common's sex workers, who had become established in 1943 when a cohort of the infamous "Piccadilly Warriors" came south to attend to the sexual needs of soldiers billeted on the Common. Trade boomed as British, Americans, Poles and any number of the other free forces assembled in SW17 ready for the big push. It was a different sort of push in the bushes and lanes of old Streatham and Tooting, as well as the Common that divided them. A few of the women liked the area so much they stayed in the neighbourhood.

For my short film, I interviewed a representative of the sex workers as well as a local councillor and a pagan practitioner, about past and present wickedness.

I began my feature with a (censored) version of my own first experience of Durexic Park. Followed gingerly by the cameraman, I strode to the pavement alongside Tooting Bec Road and dropped down into the woods. I described the darkness and muffled traffic sounds, as well as subtler ones; scurrying, sniffs, the occasional grunt or crash as a dog bounded into the bushes. The foliage of the shrubs was enlivened by bright plastic containers and a collage of torn gossip redtops and adult top shelfs.

Twigs and leaves crackled underfoot as I walked past small clearings. I stopped, turned to the camera and described how as a boy I had once been walking towards one of these clearings, off to the left near the railway tracks, when a flock of birds flew up from the far edge, just short of a denser pocket of trees with no undergrowth. My attention had been attracted by the sound of rustling and the groans of a man. Then I saw him – jogging bottoms pulled down and another figure crouched in front of him.

Looking suitably wry, I related how I'd mumbled a quick, "Sorry mate" and stumbled away down the main path. I wasn't quite sure of what I'd seen but deep down I knew. It was as if my eyes had been opened and now I saw more people on the paths and in the bushes, moving slowly past each other in what was almost a kind of dance. Young looking women, older men. Not knowing where to look, I had turned, cut across the open patches towards Garrad's Road and got the 315 bus back home.

In my piece to camera I stopped there, a nice boy frightened by a bad place and scared to go back. In reality, long after that first time, my mind stayed in the woods and I returned to them repeatedly. I think I used my early interest in journalism as cover and made the Common my first investigation; but for this short piece, I was able to find other people to speak about their experiences.

Wendy resembled a yoga instructor or proprietor of a vegan café rather than, as she described herself, a former Common woodworker. She wore soft woollens and jeans for the interview and light make-up that barely covered the hardness in her face under her blonde fringe, the result of years battling addiction and selling sex in south London. She spoke slowly.

"We've always known that there's something strange in the area. A couple of the older girls talk of a sort of monster, but one that might also defend them. During the war one woman was murdered as the troops assembled around the Common and each army suspected the others."

When I asked where she thought the "monster" came from, she answered after taking a deep breath.

"In the 1940s there was a Jewish girl, Elisheba, from Prague, who said that in her city an entity was summoned to help the community when it was in trouble. It was a being of clay, made alive through rituals and Hebrew incantations. It's thought that she brought something to life here to protect the girls."

I asked what became of Elisheba but Wendy couldn't provide a definite answer.

"No one traced Elisheba or knew what happened to her but so many people disappeared in the war. She could have married and moved to Utah. Or Usk or Uxbridge. One theory is that she sacrificed her own life to put an end to the freak she'd created."

Wendy paused before adding with a grim smile, "Only, we're still here. And maybe it is too."

The second interviewee joined the conversation at this point. Jane was educated, mixed race and cheerfully self-identified as a witch. Her clothes, if described in terms of music, would be mid-period Fleetwood Mac, with lots of floaty layers. Her contribution took the story back further, to the nineteenth century and the events at the Priory.

Jane claimed that Florence had enticed an imp into the world, part playmate and part bodyguard. Florence's first husband had been an abusive man, as had her father before him, and Florence craved a protector although Jane couldn't say – beyond alluding to several occult traditions that teach the necessary skills – how Florence created it.

Jane asserted that this imp killed both Florence's first husband and father and that it was this same fiend, reawakened, that either did for Charles Bravo directly or caused him to commit suicide. After Bravo, it was Florence who suffered and ended her days addicted to laudanum though not before she had managed to lay the horror in its grave.

I asked them both the same question:

"To clarify for our viewers. Am I right that you both think that there may have been, or still is, an unnatural creature on the Common? And if you do, I have to ask what you think it is."

Looking straight at the camera, Wendy answered first:

"I think it's an urban legend. A myth the girls tell themselves to warn each other or feel better about working the Common. A kind of super pimp, if you will."

Jane was more measured in her tone but more extreme in her answer:

"I think it's what the Jewish girl surmised it to be, a golem brought forth initially by Florence Bravo, that was killed by her and was then resurrected at various points. I'm concerned because, in the scriptures, lore and legend, there are common factors. It is brought forth of mud and word and guided by those words. The Prague one was from the word of God and Florence's from the devil. But what words might be imprinted around here?"

She gestured towards the shrubs.

"What did you see littered on the bushes, fences and trees when you first came here? What shiny printed paper is trodden down into the soil, under leaves, stuffed into nooks and crannies? Screaming tabloids, jazz mags, skin rags, often soiled with seed, are the printed words that will summon life into our Tooting Common golem."

I paused, to give viewers the time to consider what a tabloid- and porn-educated demon might be like.

Jane continued:

"I think it may regenerate by accident. It would not be fully formed – that would require conscious human will from someone like Florence or Elisheba – but all the other ingredients are here. Desperate need, printed words and a feeder stream for the Falconbrook near the railway bridge for the clay."

The final interviewee was Counsellor Kumu Chaunna in a dark blue suit with a broad chalk pinstripe, from which protruded stiff cuffs that matched his collar, a restrained, tightly fashioned tie beneath it. His manner mirrored his formal dress sense.

"There have been efforts to improve this area and remove prostitution. Balham is a family place and we at Wandsworth Council need no help from mythical monsters to clean up the neighbourhood. Moreover, broadcasting what can, at best, be described as a folk tale is likely to have a detrimental effect on house prices."

My conclusion to camera followed. I spoke of old professions, wartime legacies, oral traditions and urban legends. I ended with a recording of children reading: "If you go down to the woods today, you're in for a big surprise/If you go down to the woods today you'll never believe your eyes" as the camera panned across the setting sun to the west of the Common.

What I did not say was that in my months of teenage research, note-taking, spying, occasionally trying and sometimes providing sexual services, I saw some very strange things. On more than one occasion, I witnessed a shuffling, polysexual creature, its hour come around again, slouching towards the High Road, trying to be fully reborn.

The Heavens Over Mortlake

The Thames ceases to be a tidal monster in the soft rugby-playing belt of south west London. Eyots pop up in its midst, there are bird sanctuaries, commons, abandoned graveyards and beavers. At least there were once beavers, as we know from the Beverley Brook, which shunts its way into the Thames west of Putney and was named after the coat-providing dam builder.

My heart and home is in Surrey but my work is on the Middlesex shore and I commute on the number 22, which links the lights of Piccadilly to the distant suburban delights of Fulwell Bus Garage. I only ride a fraction of the possible route but sometimes imagine an impoverished fashion-obsessed outer London misfit making the trek back to Fulwell from the glamour, smoke and LGBTQI sanctuaries of Soho, and my own stepping-on point of Chelsea. However, I cannot tell who, if any, amongst the young clubbers, older cleaners, transport workers, men (and occasionally women) on dubious, or even desperate, missions do the whole journey.

I get off at Mortlake and sometimes snooze through the, relatively, inner stretches of Sloany Pony Parsons Green, Putney and Barnes. The route of the 22 or N22 bus is middle, if not upper, class. However, as the rich require the services of the poor, the bus passengers are more mixed socially, racially and educationally. There are fewer students since Chelsea Art College moved to Pimlico but there are some alumni, like myself, who settled into the route and gained employment on *The* King's Road. Note the capital, for it is *The*, not the. Now I am a head chef – not exactly the Brit Art dream but still a bit glam, though not so fashionable that I don't take the night bus home.

Putney is the crossing point, a borderline. In 1647 the Leveller debates were held there and the subsequent crushing of them and formation of the New Model Army did much to shape British political history, as well as provide handy names for angry musical combos. The current bridge built in 1886 by Joseph Bazalgette is successor to one built in 1729, where early feminist Mary Wollstonecroft was rescued by a passing boat when she threw herself off it. She had planned to kill herself from Battersea Bridge, but that crossing was not private enough for her purposes.

The bridges stitch together the villages on either side of the Thames, and the result is the westerly drift of London we know today, as the settlements linked up east to west alongside the river too. A city over the water grew on the south bank, away from the guilds and London's walls. That is one version. In another, the villages continue to exist as before, it's just that now there are houses in between. Each hamlet has its own myths, stories and history. Putney, as previously indicated, has an unlikely connection to revolution, and its Common has an even more improbable one to football. For there, in a neglected graveyard in a sex-hunted cruisy wood, is the grave of William Cobb Morley, the man who wrote the rules of soccer.

Putney Common is one of the more interesting stops at three in the morning as men furtively glide on, flushed with release and conquest. Barnes, on the other hand, is always a quiet stop despite its artistic and literary heritage, especially the musical greats from Handel and Holst via Tubby Hayes to Brian May and Duffy.

Next up is my stop at Mortlake, named after a shallow lake famous for spawning young salmon (mort), not a gothic death (morte). As a young goth this disappointed me but as a middle-aged chef, I'm happier to be linked to a salmon spawning ground. Mortlake is also associated with Britain's greatest magicians, Tommy Cooper and John Dee. Cooper lived nearby and was cremated there whilst Dee's grave is lost under the High Street, his old home and library built over by a modern block called "John Dee House".

Dee was a mathematician, scholar, linguist, traveller, spy, astronomer of European repute, alleged alchemist, and necromancer. Furthermore, with the aid of something called a scrye mirror and a sidekick known as Edward Kelley, Dee spoke to angels. He spent time in the Tower as a guest of "Bloody" Mary Tudor, indicted as a heretic while his home was the target of religious mobs who hurled fire and biblical quotes. It amuses me to think that, should such an event reoccur today, some of that mob might travel to it using the 22 bus.

Years of taking the route myself has made me nosy. Whilst I rarely speak to any of the passengers it is possible to learn a great deal from overheard phone calls, reading matter, posture and clothing. What I like to refer to as "my" regulars include the clever girl in woollen tights, who clearly has a terribly important, possibly medical-related, job. There are also the Somali mum, who I assume is employed in the office cleaning sector because that's what my prejudices tell me, the nervous Ghanaian, the jolly pensioner and a young man I imaginatively call "Emo". Emo works in a West End bar but we haven't communicated yet beyond the weary smile fellow commuters sometimes exchange.

They probably do the same with me; dark skinned chef with a Yorkshire accent who could stand to lose a few pounds. They might note how my sober, or alcohol lit, reading, window gazing and phone-game playing switches to a nervy manner on the evenings one of the restaurant patrons passes me a line of what he insists on calling "Gianluca Vialli."

One night, no doubt inadvertently, he slipped me an altogether more illuminating class A and I became aware of this on the journey home. It was late spring and the trees twinkled with promise as the street lights brought the new leaf into beautiful relief. Crossing Putney Bridge, I noticed an extra effervescence as the Thames reflected the shimmering lights of the traffic and I wondered idly how long the trip would last.

With my new-found drug-fuelled empathy, the clever girl in the woollen tights looked to be in a bit of a bad way. I couldn't tell what was bothering her and I never got close to finding out because that's when I saw the first one. A chap with a neat little moustache, gelled hair greying at the temples and a nice herring bone jacket, who was sitting in front of the girl, seemed to be whispering to her. Initially I was a bit jealous, then intrigued, and finally outraged. Before I could do anything she got up for her stop and he vanished. Next thing I knew he was sitting at the front of the bus adjacent to an elderly man who seemed to be listening and responding with smiles.

Slightly spooked, I looked about.

The upper deck had half a dozen people in front of me and a couple behind, gently trying to make the journey home as comfortable as possible. I glanced towards the stairs and was unable to avert my eyes from a tall man in a shabby, once expensive, overcoat. I gave him an involuntary nod, but then he broke all bus etiquette and strode up to me, took the seat in front of me and stared.

I blinked and was about to say something when he asked, "You can see me?"

I nodded. Then he indicated the man beside the old man and

asked, "And Anael?"

I concurred again so he pointed out a blonde woman with a kindly face who I'd not noticed before.

"Yes."

He smiled. It was a smile that cheered me and put my troubles in perspective.

He laughed, a low gentle laugh, and said that it had been some time since he'd had a proper chat. And there we were, having a proper chat about politics, the weather, Fulham's chances of avoiding relegation and the merits, or otherwise, of local restaurants. He deferred to me when he learned my profession, and he spoke of ambiance and mood rather than the actual food.

I nearly missed my stop but I had to ask, even though I thought I knew the answer. What was he?

"Me?" He pointed to himself. "Us?" he gestured round to the others. "We are angels of course. We like to help the sad and poorly, offer them comfort. I think Oriel" he gestured to the woman, "has had soft words with you in the past."

"But why here? Why this place?"

He grinned and said, "We've been on this bit of the river, Mortlake and Chiswick, since the great magician spoke to us. He taught us many things and great wisdom."

Here the angel leaned over closer and whispered, "He told us of future events and news. He said that when the police arrested two kids, one for drinking battery acid and the other for eating fireworks, they charged one and let the other one off."

Then he disappeared. Just like that.

Karlene at the Crossroads

When I was in primary school we used to sing a song that went "Look in the mirror and what do I see? A big nothing threatening me." My siblings would tease me by changing the words to "a big something" (elder sisters) or "a big Neville" (younger brother, using my name).

My character was defined early and I always felt I was being threatened, either by something else or by myself. I didn't think my siblings were responsible. Besides, what was it about the eighties and songs about mirrors?

These days, mirror in the bathroom aside, I avoided the mirror man and you could bet your bottom dollar I'd do anything to distract myself from facing the truth when staring into one. Remembering and punning songs was just one such tactic as I steered the razor beneath nose (too beaky), around cheeks (too red), below ears (too sticky outty) and along chin (too weak). Some mornings I considered hitting myself with an actual frying pan rather than go through the mental battering I gave myself. This would have had the additional advantage of leaving bruising that would distract from skin colour (too pale and blotchy), skin texture (too greasy) and eyes (too alert).

All this would take place every morning, after my night's broken slumber and before I left for work.

I'm not exactly sure how I found out about Autonomous Sensory Meridian Response, or ASMR to the cognoscenti. It may have been accidentally while trawling the web or in a radio documentary, but as soon as I tried it I knew I had found a good thing, and when I found her I was entranced. Her appealing accent and the sense that she knew about suffering, had seen injustice and people being mistreated sang out to me. My own manifold losses, rejections and resentments against slights, real and imagined, made me immediately sympathetic towards her.

She projected strength gained through misfortune and a message that living was worthwhile. This sang to me because within my tin of depression I felt that, compared to others, my life contained less joy and I deserved fewer pleasures. I had been questioning why I should carry on.

120

It certainly wasn't for the precarious job in Lambeth social services that just about covered my rent and food. Was it the hope of getting better or meeting someone special?

Maybe she *was* the special one.

I'm not certain I can accurately describe how ASMR helped but it did. Listening to a woman speak kindly and softly as I carried out mundane chores soothed me. For the short period of the recording, my troubles vanished into the bubble of whispered tenderness where I felt, not happiness exactly, but calm. It complemented my medical regime and, despite my doctor's scepticism and fear that I might have a relapse, resulted in a reduction of my pill intake. My employers were not supportive, even though ASMR guided me through the more demanding aspects of my job.

Another reason I specifically liked Karlene – there, I've said her name – was that she talked about her own occupations and their challenges. It was never clear whether she was still employed but she was evidently bright, sensitive and caring and, from what I gleaned from the videos, the jobs she did were obviously beneath her. There was a fierce pride in her, too, and it shone through that, despite all the hardships, she would survive. This inspired me to keep going.

The videos kept me going out of the door, past the disappointment of anonymous mail, witchdoctor flyers, political rants, magazines, addressed to the tenant, the legal occupier, 176A, 176C or, just occasionally, 174C. Down the steps to the street and the short walk to the bus stop that was already prickly with elbows, umbrellas and schoolchildren. Schoolchildren could smell vulnerability at a hundred yards and were rarely shy in sharing such an observation.

That day was a good day. The bus came quickly. I found a seat and sat back, turned on my music and stared out of the window.

When I saw *her* it was like a jolt of electricity pulsing into me. I couldn't believe it was really her!

To see Karlene from the bus, in the howling mediocrity of Streatham of all places, was incredible. Perhaps I should have picked up on clues earlier in the subjects she spoke about but, to be honest, her words often washed over me. It was the intonation that mattered. The soft throaty whisper as she folded and unfolded paper, gently wrapping whatever object she had to hand with stiff brown paper and string. Her voice rasped gently and seductively and her laughter came easily as she bubbled away merrily, the warmth of somewhere exotic in her tone.

Yet there she was. At eye level with the top deck. Standing on a balcony, staring out and across the road, almost looking through the number 109. I twisted my head to watch her receding into the distance as the bus began its descent down Brixton Hill.

If the reception on my phone was better I would have checked immediately but when I logged on at work I knew the recording had been made in the place I'd seen her. She was wearing knee-high boots, a suede skirt with a white shirt, and a red kerchief tied round her neck. Her words seemed angrier than before. She spoke of wrapping but now it was wringing that her hands were doing, over and over. Like Lady Macbeth obsessively washing her hands whilst the words tumbled out. Staccato, slow, full of a slight contempt, instilling both pity and rage in the listener.

> *In one shop, they made me use cardboard. Thin cardboard but too stiff to mould. I'd just lost my dear pet dog but they paid no attention to my suffering; even when my hands bled the bully boss told me to carry on. So I did. Bleeding and folding, folding and bleeding till my time came to report him, though he deserved more than a disciplinary. I'd have taken the blunt scissors we had to remove what in his opinion made him male, and I'd have sent them off with an order. That's what they made me do, put heavy objects into paper and parcel them up. Heavy objects that made my wrists hurt, heavy objects that harmed my joints, cardboard paper that cut my hand and dust that irritated my nose and made me ill.*
>
> *None of this was in my job description, none of it but they made me do it. They had no respect. He had no respect.*
>
> *He used to.*
>
> *He used to want me like all real men want me, he used to hang onto my words, he used to listen like you do, like you and the many others.*
>
> *One time I saw him aching to touch me.*
>
> *As if I'd let him.*
>
> *Touch me!*

I jerked away from the screen. Feelings of guilt and desire flooded my brain. I still had the old response – that I was being supported –

but this was also darker and more disturbing. Not just how I interpreted what Karlene was saying but how I had initially (mis)interpreted her words. I felt that this was a personal message directed at me and me alone, and that the *"Touch me!"* was a command.

My heart was aflutter, and my stomach flipped in anticipation as I got on the number 109 at Brixton for the journey home. I was also fearful that there would be no available seats on the top deck, and started making up stories in case I needed to coax people away from a place at the west side window. Fortunately, there was an empty seat six rows back, which I bustled my way to.

I counted the stops, panting, almost repeating them like an incantation after the polite voice of the bus announcer read them out.

Rush Common, Blenheim Gardens, Jebb Avenue (alight for Brixton Prison), New Park Road, Holmewood Road and finally (thank Christ!), Christchurch Road.

Her building became visible as the bus crested the hill but when I saw the drawn curtains and empty balcony I felt crushed. I considered getting off and waiting outside the flat for a glimpse of her. However, that would be psychotic, and also the most obvious viewing spot – a patch of council gardening and scrub bench – was already occupied by a group of what looked like street drinkers.

I had a full evening's online viewing ahead and ate my supper hunched over my elderly Dell laptop.

I began with the most recent video and then moved to a kind of subsection I'd found, entitled Dark Karlene.

In the first of these, again about employment, she was wearing the white shirt and red scarf (in her hair this time) and from the brief full shots I could see she appeared to be wearing black leggings. I did sometimes jealously ponder whether there was a cameraman or woman involved as the videos were expertly done and cleanly edited.

*It wasn't that they didn't know my potential. It was rather that they wilfully chose to ignore it and set me to do trivial tasks. They had me prepare posters and design leaflets yet had the temerity to alter the words I'd written. Words that **I had** chosen. Words that communicated **meaning** to the enlightened. Words of wisdom and encouragement to those who wished to* *hear. But no, they rejected **my words** because they weren't inclusive enough, they weren't precise enough, the language was the **wrong** level.*

At this point the folding became, briefly, more frantic and the camera moved to Karlene's face so that one could just see what looked like old scars under the make-up. The close-up became softer, the scars dissolved, and the monologue continued.

I'm only interested in one level. I'm only interested in one clarity and I only include those who wish to be included. I only want the intelligent, the sensitive and the devoted.

The camera panned rapidly out and back, producing a strange effect where it appeared that she had four arms. Two up, open and welcoming; two others with scissors from which dripped a red ribbon.

I gave them simpleton guides once. Guides for idiots, a fool's guide, but they rejected those as well, saying they were too simple and patronising. So I was rejected for being too simple. After this I vowed to just give them the truth.

She followed this with one of the incantations that featured in many of her videos and were another reason I was attracted to her over other ASMR practitioners. I managed to write down an approximation of one of them. It ran, "I offer nothing in return but in devotion you will find peace".

On a fan site called "Dark Karlene's yogic chants in English" I discovered more, including the following:

Can mercy be found in the heart of she who was born of stone?
Was she not merciless, would she kick the breast of her lord?
Men call you merciful, but there is no trace of mercy in you.
You have cut off the heads of the children of others, and these you wear as a garland around your neck.
It matters not how much I call you. You hear me, but you will not listen.

I wondered what horrors she had been through to find succour in these chants and, more alarmingly, the comfort and indeed abandonment I found in them. I felt an overwhelming, unconditional love whatever her indifference to my wellbeing might be. It would be glorious to suffer, bring my desires to nothing and ruin such belongings as I had. Her good was all.

It gave me purpose and felt liberating. I took up yoga and began following Karlene's lessons. I meditated at home, on the bus and at work. I altered my diet and ordered some special ghee from one of the sites devoted to her. I didn't like the taste, but I found the chanting calmed me down, blocked bad feelings and encouraged me to concentrate. I started out with *Um Klim Kalika-yei Namaha* but then I found another, one that came with warnings attached.

It was on a website that cautioned that the mantra would eradicate bits of myself that I thought were acceptable. But here's the thing: there was no part of me I was determined to hold on to! The site added that using the chant would lead to an intense, unnerving, probably uncomfortable, certainly disruptive experience. There was nothing new in any of that for me, so I started saying it.

Om Hrim Shreem Klim Adya Kalika Param Eshwari Swaha

My days changed. Everything altered.

The people I shared the house with stopped avoiding me, and shopkeepers and colleagues became more polite. My sisters and brother did not bother to disguise their relief at the improvements in my appearance and confidence. I swear my sister-in-law even made a pass at me at the Christmas get-together. My sisters talked of setting me up with someone; but I, of course, already had someone.

I was assiduous in watching the videos as they were posted. Sometimes they seemed to be intended specifically for me, at others they were more general. One instruction in January was explicit. I was to cut my hair very short and cut myself, on the arm, very deeply. I didn't think not to, I just immersed myself in the task, did my yoga and upped my devotions. A couple of women from the shared house joked about joining my yoga sessions and asked where I learned it. They were impressed when I told them. In the past, I would have been proud of that but now I just calmly accepted my new status. I felt that I could achieve anything.

So when the next personal instruction came in, I was ready.

It was terrible and simple. I was to murder a man employed at the Tate Library Brixton. I was given a date, Tuesday 12th of March, and a method, strangulation. I was instructed on the means of entry and exit to the building and given three weeks to plan. I started right away. There was no question of not doing it and, above all, *she* promised to wave me off.

When the day came, I was focused. I strode to the top deck and firmly requested that a young lad taking up two seats moved to make room. I made sure I sat next to the window and stared out as the stops rolled by.

Ederline Avenue, *Om Hrim Shreem Klim Adya Kalika Param Eshwari Swaha.*

Tylecroft Road, *Om Hrim Shreem Klim Adya Kalika Param Eshwari Swaha.*

Norbury Station, Hermitage Lane, Arragon Gardens, Kempshott Road, *Om Hrim Shreem Klim Adya Kalika Param Eshwari Swaha.*

Greyhound Lane, Streatham Station, St Leonard's Church, Becmead Avenue, Kingscourt Road, Mount Ephraim Road, Streatham Hill Station, Barrhill Road, Telford Avenue, *Om Hrim Shreem Klim Adya Kalika Param Eshwari Swaha.*

Finally, Christchurch Road.

She wore the white blouse, and untied the red neckerchief as I approached and waved it. I felt like a knight going into battle for his lady. I was supercharged, invincible and, truly for the first time, full of resolve.

In my lunch break I marched across to the library to check everything was in order. I was confident I could access the staff side entrance and the exits from the main floor to the offices where he would be. It was all as she said. When I returned in the evening, armed with a scarf and bolt, it was a simple matter of slipping into the office, quickly slinging the rumāl around the man's neck and pulling. The blood rush in my ears and hymns of devotion in my head rather wiped out any sounds he might have made. It was over in moments and soon I was out of the side exit. My heart was light. I felt achievement and peace and enlightenment.

If only I'd known it was this easy.

I walked around the church and up St Matthew's Road through the estate, which was the swiftest way to the hill, and up past Raleigh Gardens. Once I might have been nervous about taking this more dangerous route. Now nothing mattered except reaching her.

Below her balcony I could see six men and two women, performing a kind of folding action with their hands. As I approached one of them glanced up at me and said, "Welcome brother."

I did feel very welcome on this blasted crossroads on the A23, especially when I saw the scar on his left arm. It was faded but had the same provenance as my own.

He led a prayer and they all joined in.

Thou art fond of cremation grounds; so I have turned my heart into one.

That thou, a resident of cemeteries, may dance there unceasingly.

O Mother! I have no other fond desire in my heart; fire of a funeral pyre is burning there;

O Mother! I have preserved the ashes of dead bodies all around that Thou may come.

The heart must become a burial ground, Pride, selfishness, and desire all broken into dust, Then, and then alone, will the Mother dance there!

I looked up and there on the balcony a figure danced, and I remembered a line from one of the fan sites. Oh Kāli Karlene, whoever on Tuesday night, having uttered thy mantra, makes offering once with devotion to thee becomes a great poet, a Lord of the earth, and ever goes mounted upon an elephant.

Such was my enchantment that I actually looked for one.

A Year from the Provinces

The view from the top deck of the number 35 differed to that of twelve months earlier. The hulking London Park Hotel and the trimmer form of the Ministry of Salsa had both vanished. Before long, the massive Heygate Estate would be gone as well. Only a handful of its hundreds of flats remained unshuttered. But Clive was still in there. At least, what was left of him was, thumping around the eighth and ninth floors. The word was, via friends of the cleaners and other council workers, that even the most hardened white pipers now avoided the top floors. The whole structure looked unsound to me and I had an image of Clive honeycombing the innards of the block, slithering through the central water and heating systems.

This was a different Clive Harper to the one Uncle Carl had sent to meet me from the train the year previously. It was only a few hundred yards' walk from the station to Uncle Carl's flat, which I was to look after for a year, but I'd been glad to see Clive. The train to the Elephant and Castle had snaked through some of the biggest, nastiest and most imposing housing schemes in the country, from which I got a real sense of the brooding power, terror and immensity of London.

"Take it all in," Clive had said, gesturing at the shopping centre and the blocks that surrounded it. "It's all going to go. Not as quickly as when the Luftwaffe did it the last time, mind."

Clive was in his twenties, younger than my uncle by more than a decade, and he still hadn't lost his native Cornish accent. However, he had acquired what Uncle Carl referred to as London Elm's Disease, a mania for London trivia that afflicts urbanites of a certain type. In the short jaunt up the Walworth Road, I learned where Michael Caine's family had lived and that, for a time, their neighbour was the painter and magician Austin Osman Spare. That Baldwins, the oldest apothecary and herbalist in London, had moved a few hundred yards to its current location opposite the plaque to Charles Babbage. Babbage was one of a triumvirate of local luminaries who had made it into the BBC's top 100 Britons, Charlie Chaplin and Michael Faraday being the others.

"SE17 had more people in that top 100 than any other postcode in the country," said Clive. "And let's not get started on Rio

Ferdinand buying a flat here, eh?" He gestured to a new housing development as we turned onto Amelia Street. "Don't want to put you off, do we?"

Uncle Carl had left on his travels the previous week so Clive showed me round the flat and told me that he lived in the next stair and that I was to call if I needed anything. He added that my uncle's mate, Sal, lived over on Peacock Street, and she was almost certain to drop by.

They were both very good about introducing me around the area but I was closer in age to Clive so spent more time with him. I certainly never went clubbing with Sal.

I didn't go that much with Clive either, and once I'd settled into my internship off Farringdon Road I found myself seduced by the bars and clubs of Clerkenwell and Holborn. Clive took me on a brief tour of some of the older pubs around there and showed me how to get out of the Inns of Court at night, but I could tell he never really felt comfortable north of the river. His speciality was inaccessible South London dives.

He came round one Saturday, just as Doctor Who was finishing, glanced at the TV, and said, "They filmed loads of this series on the Brandon Estate up the road, you know."

I did know, as it happened, but I was startled by what he said next.

"Bunch of us are going to Ministry of Salsa tonight. Fancy coming?"

Until then, the closest I'd got to the Ministry of Salsa (or Cheney's, its grimmer rival) had been to watch a fight out the back one summer evening, between thirty or so Latin Americans armed with scaffolding poles. I sipped my tea and said, "You gave me the impression that salsa was for further education workers with limited dance skills, and that the Ministry of Salsa was the very apotheosis of a dreadful night out." In truth, Cheney's was worse as the chances of being a victim of knife, or indeed gun, crime were appreciably higher there.

"Yeah but it's closing tonight isn't it?"

I'd been in London long enough to know that, for sufferers of London Elm's Disease, nothing, but nothing, makes an event special like the last time a place is open to the public. Dorothy Parker once sniffed about people who would turn up to the opening of an envelope. If she lived in London today she would have been gifted the opportunity to be equally dismissive of those who would arrive for the closing of a book.

So I said, "Yeah, sure, what time?"

Clive, myself and two acquaintances of his, Tony and Maria both originally from Belfast, took the back route towards the Draper Estate. Clive tried to impress me with his local knowledge, this time about Newington Butts, which turned out not to be a reference to water collection or arse exposure but a place where archery was, and still can be, practiced. Thankfully, no one was improving their arrow skills or even playing basketball in the sunken court behind the club as we joined the short queue. As our group descended to the coat check I noticed a huge tank, which was empty save for some wood and a few bits of greenery. I mentioned this to Tony, and he shrugged.

"Looks like it might be for a reptile. Used to be a pet shop about here, huge place. Maybe it's left over from that." As Maria checked her coat she said that she remembered the shop too. Then she smiled at me and said, "Do you dance?"

Maria and I drifted on and off the dance floor and, and I spent a decent amount of time keeping some of the slipperier clientele away from her. After a while, I spotted Clive with a gorgeous woman and waved them over to a booth we had just secured.

Up close, the woman was even more stunning. Lithe, Latino, grey eyes that flickered with a lazy fire as if they had trapped heat inside them. Her hair was shortish and crafted up in a crest. She wore pale-coloured boots that looked as if they might be snakeskin, and a matching belt over her tan dress.

She held out her hand and said, "Eve, Eve Pedrevan, how do you do?"

"Maria. And this is James," she said, indicating me. "James Onbeschoft. I guess you've met Clive?"

"Clive?" said Eve. "I thought he was saying Cleave! Must be his accent. You know him well?"

"Well enough," said Maria. "James here knows him better."

Eve turned to me and her eyes flared into life, briefly.

"Maria? Fancy a tab?" said Clive, rising from his seat. "We'll leave you two non-addicts to get acquainted."

"So," I said, once the pair had disappeared in the direction of smokers' corner. "You like Clive's dancing?"

She laughed and said, "I think he moves like an asthmatic

panda."

"Is that a phrase from your own country?"

"No, it's a phrase from here. No one dances that badly where I'm from." She sipped her drink and added, "I think your friend Clive wishes to sleep with me."

I blushed. "Yes I expect he does." I would have continued, but she held a finger to my lips and said, "Listen. You must do all you can to stop that happening. It will be very, very bad for him if he does."

I suggested that she could stop him, but she said again that I must try. I put a list of questions to her. Did she not like him? Find him attractive? Was she married, engaged? A criminal? A murderer? She laughed at all of these. I asked if she had a disease; she shook her head and said, "No, not in the sense you mean. But if he sleeps with me, Clive will change."

I bet he will, I thought. I promised I would try to do as she asked but could easily imagine Clive's response, even though I could honestly say I wasn't jealous, as there was something about Eve I found disturbing, almost as if there was a bit of herself she was scared of.

Later in the evening, I did try to talk to Clive. All he said was that he'd never forced anyone to do anything and he wasn't about to start now. I shrugged and told him Eve had asked me to speak to him, at which point things got a little tense, but then Maria appeared and I was happy to turn my focus to her.

As the club closed for the last time, we all left together. At Amelia Street I made a last effort, a half-hearted offer of coffee at mine, but Clive and Eve swept on and Maria looked at me askance.

"I wouldn't have had you down as a group man," she smirked as we fell through the door together.

The next day, we made our way back to the Ministry to retrieve Maria's jacket, which she'd neglected to pick up from the coat check. As we descended I noticed that the tank was now occupied by a lizard.

A text arrived from Clive: 'Bloody typical of you. Go to a salsa club and get off with an Irish girl.' A day later he texted again and asked me to go round to his flat. I was barely through the door when he started with odd, seemingly unrelated, questions about Eve. At last, looking very embarrassed, he told me he thought he might have caught something.

"Like what?"

"Well. Some sort of growth hormone, by the looks of it."

"Did you get me round here so you could brag?" I said. "You realise that half of all the emails ever sent offer penis enlargement, millions of pounds are spent trying to achieve it and you're complaining about it? Perhaps it's just Eve," I laughed. "Perhaps it hasn't calmed down yet."

"It is just Eve, and she warned me," he said. I waited for him to say more, and recalled what Eve had said to me. Clive went on, "Eve suggested that, after her, I might not want to sleep with anyone else again. I thought she was just talking dirty. You know. Priming me for a treat." He paused. "It was a treat by the way, a really unforgettable time but this..." he touched his groin, "this is not arousal. It's physical. I've acquired what the Aussies call a zipper ripper."

"So you don't regret all of it?"

"Oh no. She was so supple, and her tongue! It seemed to grow to three times normal length."

I could see how that might be useful but wasn't sure I needed more details.

"She didn't stay over then?"

"No. She woke me up early and said she had to go. No idea where she lives or anything. And I can't go back to the club now because it's closed."

I told him how we'd returned to the club and seen the lizard in the tank. Now I thought about it, its skin looked very similar to Eve's boots.

"They'll be selling off the effects probably. If you wanted a souvenir."

"Very funny. How's Maria?"

With hindsight, that was the last normal conversation I had with Clive. The following week, Sal and I went to see him, but he didn't bother to say anything, just slapped what looked like a French stick on the table.

Sal gasped, before she regained her composure and said, "Well, there would be a living to be made in Vauxhall with that."

Clive ignored her and said it was a good job baggy clothes were fashionable because it was hampering his movement. "But not," he added mysteriously, "its own. I know it sounds like I'm going mental, and that's what the doctors think, but I believe it goes off by itself."

"Yeah. I've heard people say that sort of thing before," Sal chipped in brightly.

He ignored her, and went on, "Odd things have been happening, and not just here." Clive indicated a cat flap that hadn't been used for years. "That was open last night. And the night before, Lisa from your stair asked me if I knew of anyone with a pet snake. She said her cat had hissed at something on the balcony that slithered away."

I had to stop him there. "Wait a minute. You think your trouser serpent has taken to wandering off on its own and chasing pussy?"

"Literally and metaphorically. Yes. Yes I do. I heard a scream from the Polish girl at number 145 the other night and when I woke up my kimono dragon was missing."

An odd image came to me from a childhood holiday in Spain, an image of a lizard losing its tail and the tail continuing to move. But I didn't think they could re-attach themselves.

"You must have dreamed it," said Sal, "Classic castration dream, I'd say, stemming from fear of commitment."

"I'm more afraid of being committed," was Clive's reply.

In the days that followed the gossip kettle started to bubble. Everyone was talking about the rumours of a creature in the area. "Pullen's serpent", it was dubbed.

By the Friday, the board outside George's Newsagent was screaming, "*Residents Add-er-nough*". I was already feeling apprehensive as I opened the South London Press. It had relegated a murder in Camberwell to page three to cover the story of the serpent. Theories abounded, and it had given column inches to all of them. One suggestion was that it had been lying dormant in a cocoon since the zoo on nearby Pasley Park had closed a century before, and had been roused by the recent building work. An old lady reported it had knocked at her door; other people had seen it come in through windows, cat flaps and letter boxes. Pet owners told of strange behaviour from their animals, which had become reluctant to enter the park at night. Valerie Lache, a photographer with a studio in Peacock Yard, managed to get a great shot of it as it disappeared over a wall. The experts who examined the photograph estimated the reptile to be more than five feet in length.

I rushed round to Clive's and knocked. Nothing. I tried his letter box but it was nailed shut. A neighbour let me onto the balcony and told me that he'd heard lots of banging coming from there over the last few days and said he hadn't seen Clive at all.

At the back, the door and windows were sealed and covered. Even the cat flap was shut tight. I tried Clive's phone and mobile, I texted, emailed and hammered on the door. Eventually, he texted back:

"Help me. The bloody thing's still getting out somehow. I'm going to have to move. Can you be here at nine? Bring Sal."

Later, we arrived as instructed. We heard bolts being drawn and a dismantling of the elaborate measures Clive had constructed to foil his skivvies lizard. He emerged looking drawn, wild and undernourished, and awkwardly holding an army kitbag against his chest. It wasn't hard to guess what it contained.

"Folded over three times," he said. "In case you're interested." Sal and I exchanged glances. The kitbag was nearly three feet long itself.

Clive indicated a rucksack and a holdall. "If you could pick up my, ah, more conventional baggage I'd be grateful," he said. "I seem to have my hands full."

I took the rucksack and Sal the holdall. "Where to?" she asked.

"The Heygate Estate. You see, I've been thinking about the effect I've been having on the neighbourhood. I must admit I've been a bit of a prick. I need somewhere to hide until I can figure out a solution, if there is one, and I'm clearly a menace to be around. I need somewhere with a lot of space where I don't care about the neighbours and won't be bothered by anyone. Where better than the Heygate? The regular citizens have been shifted from the top floors and I'm sure the junkie squatters won't call the police."

"Will you be able to get in?"

"Oh, he can get in and out of anywhere."

I was disturbed that Clive referred to it as something separate from himself, but people who refer to their dicks as "old fellow" or "John Thomas" always disturb me.

Clive saw my face and said, "I've been reading up on this. I've become contaminated." Here, he did a remarkably good impersonation of Ian Paisley. "These also shall be unclean unto you among the creeping things that creep upon the earth; the weasel, and the mouse, and the tortoise after his kind. And the ferret, and the chameleon, and the lizard, and the snail, and the mole." He paused and laughed. "Jews really hate snakes, the only animal undeserving of pity. Other cultures say you should use your enemy's hand to catch a snake. That's what I'm thinking of. I'm thinking of the scaggies in there."

The three of us marched raggedly towards the Heygate and made our way to the seventh floor. Clive turned to us and said, "Well. I guess this is it. Kill or cure. If I don't see you again, I'd like to impart one bit of wisdom to you. Never, ever, no matter how much you want to do it, sleep with a beautiful woman with lizard skin boots."

He hugged Sal as best he could and twisted off down the corridor.

****

Looking at the Heygate from the bus, it was impossible to tell which part of the building he was in. The sun glinted off the top floors as Maria and I turned to face each other. The number 35 weaved and curved its way north through Borough towards London Bridge then over the water far away from SE17 and the strangeness it contained.

Notes and Comments

The Hellraiser bus stop in the **Introduction** gained its name after video tapes of the film Hellraiser repeatedly appeared on top of the bus shelter. The Peckham Terminator was the name given to a young, angry man who walked through the glass doors of a parked bus at Nigel Road Peckham.

Liebe Astrid is a reference to the former Red Army Faction member Astrid Proll, who lived incognito for a time in London. London nerd types might have clocked the use of *Smoke Magazine*'s description of the P5's "low centre of gravity".

The narrator of **The Lad Who Walked Alone** is incorrect when he suggests Mrs Thatcher was the originator of the phrase "men taking the bus over a certain age have failed in life". She is popularly credited with it but the quote is more accurately linked to Lady Lindsey of Downhill (also known as Lady Loelia of Westminster). However, when asked, Loelia, said she had taken it from English writer Brian Howard. As a side note, Lady Lil was also the basis for James Bond's secretary, Loelia "Lil" Ponsonby, who features in four of Ian Fleming's spy series. Brian Howard was, in part, the influence for pretty much any camp character Evelyn Waugh wrote about, most notably Anthony Blanche in *Brideshead Revisited.*

In the same story, the lines from the poem at the end are from *London* by William Blake, who wrote it, and the better known *Jerusalem*, about the transformation in his lifetime of parts of the Surrey shore from semi-rural to predominantly urban and industrial.

Anyone wishing to find the exact location of Catford's lost film studios from **The Tale of the Raven and of the Kat** might be confused by references to them being in Southend.

This is not Southend on the Essex coast but a now vanished suburb of Catford itself, which was home not only to the film industry but also a well-supported football club called Catford Southend, who were nicknamed The Kittens.

Some liberties have been taken with the timelines in this story as strictly speaking the main theatre of Catford did not overlap with the film studies. There is, however, a project similar to the one described and I'm grateful to the real Helena from Brockwell Lido for telling me about the Alzheimer's project she worked on, which inspired the **Tale of the Raven and of the Kat**.

Liberties too have been taken in **Sound of the Suburbs**. During the period the narrator (Nigel) was growing up, the venue that became Caesars in 1995 would have been the Ritzy from 1990 and before that the Studio (1984 to 1990). In 1969 it was the Cat's Whiskers Club, where the Rolling Stones, Small Faces and Rod Stewart performed on its revolving stage and where both Miss World and Come Dancing were hosted. More intriguing is the urban legend that the ghost of Ruth Ellis, who briefly worked at the venue, haunts the site.

Also in **Sound of the Suburbs**, Nigel quotes a polite version of the "Sutton for mutton" rhyme. Another working can be found in *The Dictionary of Proverbs* by George Latimer Apperson, which runs, "Sutton for mutton/Carshalton for beeves/Epsom for whores/and Ewel for thieves".

There is an extract from Rudyard Kipling's *The River's Tale* in the **Commodore of the Pepys Estate** but little evidence that the idea of Jolly Roger pirate flag originated at St Nicholas Church. It is, however, the closest church to the dockyards, from where those sailing out of London would be provisioned.

Folk music types may have picked up on the reworking of the Ewan MacColl song *Sweet Thames* in **Sung by the Neck**, and folkloric sorts might recognise the Scandinavian and

Saxon versions of the legend of the waterhorse, known in Northern Europe as the Neck or Neckar.

There is an unintentional irony in the fact that **A Gold for Big Ben** starts in the Carnegie Library; since the story was first written, the garden in which the narrator relaxes has been turned into a gym.

I Thought We Was Fam owes much to the *Stepford Wives* by Ira Levin including the name Dis "Dee" Coba.

The quote ("Love, from its very nature, must be transitory") near the end of **The Liberty Bus** is from Mary Wollstonecraft's *A Vindication of the Rights of Woman*, published in 1792. This is included partly because it is germane to the story but also because the RV bus passed just north of Mary's former home off the Blackfriars Road.

The recently discontinued RV1 route was a popular one with visitors as it linked several of London's top tourist attractions: Somerset House, the Royal Festival Hall, the Globe, Borough Market, Tower Bridge and the Tower of London. Less obvious to the tourist is that is passed through many of the old liberties. These were autonomous areas outside the authority of the City of London with their own laws and tax regimes; for example, prostitution was legal in the South Bank liberties from Paris Gardens to the Clink. The end point, Tower Hill, was the liberty of the Mint.

The story of Queen Rat is unique to London and comes from the toshers who scavenged in the sewers and buried rivers. The most recent example of someone claiming that a relative of theirs had spent a night of passion with Ms Rat was in the 1920s.

Jeux Sans Frontier was inspired by a storytelling performance by Vanessa Woolf-Hoyle on the old Surrey Canal. I'm extremely grateful to Vanessa and also Taro Tsuruta of Tsuruta Architects who turned the story into a piece of installation art called *The Peckham Toymaker* for the 2017 London Festival of Architecture.

The plot of **The Heavens Over Mortlake** borrows from Wim Wenders' film, *Der Himmel über Berlin,* but contains more bus travel and Tommy Cooper jokes than the original.

The quote about unclean creatures in **A Year from the Provinces** is taken from the Bible, Leviticus 11:29.

Versions of **Bank Holiday Weekend**, **Having a Bubble**, **A Year from the Provinces** and **Keep Smiling Through** first appeared in issues 4, 5, 6 and 7 of the twenty-first century Penny Dreadful, *One Eye Grey.*

Synopsis of stories

The Last of the Gang to Die – An emotional return to Shooter's Hill for one of the original dandy highwaymen.

A Cyborg's Dream of the P13 – On the buses with a cyborg fan of one of South London's most meandering routes.

Liebe Astrid – A tale of exile off Coldharbour Lane.

White Man on the Clapham Omnibus – He never thought it would happen on a bus that runs through Clapham.

The Lad Who Walked Alone – They've shut the sex sauna and made the area la-di-da and things ain't what they used to be.

New Cross Roads and Friendly Streets – One woman's search for love, meaning and political correctness on the way to Lewisham.

The Tale of the Raven and of the Kat – Hollywood glamour and foreign nobility on the banks of the Ravensbourne.

Sound of the Suburbs – Bus travel through some South London suburbs as a mindfulness technique.

Commodore of the Pepys Estate – A retired pirate gains a national treasure money cannot buy.

Fruit and Nuts – Sex, drugs and rock and roll and picking fruit by the Pool River.

Having a Bubble – London is a mirror in all things and we see things differently depending on which side of the looking glass we are on.

Bank Holiday Weekend – Revenge can be a dish served damp and windy.

Sung by the Neck – Not all buskers are quite what they seem. Not all buses, either, come to that.

Keep Smiling Through – Adults tell children there are no monsters. Most of the time, this is true.

A Gold for Big Ben – A journalist finds himself well and truly sucker-punched in this sporting comeback tale.

I Thought We Was Fam – It's not easy for young hearts to run free in the "roaring twenties".

Jeux Sans Frontier – A tale of cruelty and hidden treasure on the banks of the Old Surrey Canal.

The Liberty Bus – The cats are there for a reason but what are they protecting us from?

Slouching to Balham High Road – The Priory broods over the West Streatham woods like a ruined pimp.

The Heavens over Mortlake – A chef finds that the doors of perception can be opened using an Oyster Card.

Karlene at the Crossroads – The top of Streatham Hill provides the solution for all of life's problems for one bus traveller.

A Year from the Provinces –The number 35 weaved and curved its way north through Borough towards London Bridge then over the water, far away from SE17 and the strangeness it contained.